Craving of the Witch

Crypt Witch cozy paranormal mystery series - book 14

K.E. O'Connor

K.E. O'Connor Books

CRAVING OF THE WITCH

ISBN: 978-1-915378-12-5

Written by: K.E. O'Connor

Chapter 1

"Has that cage got a silver coating?" I squinted, a scowl on my face, as an enormous cage was hoisted off the back of a delivery truck at the bottom of the hill leading to the stone circle.

Wiggles' eyes glowed red. "They'd better not be interested in catching a hellhound."

"I don't think they're looking for you. That cage is meant for something huge." My bad mood deepened as the cage was set on wheels and moved away by four burly guys.

"Hey, Tempest. I see you're taking in the show." Tate Rathmore strolled over, his usually cheerful face pensive. He held a pizza box in his hands.

"Hi, Tate. I can't believe this is happening." I gestured at the four trucks and the gaggle of people milling about.

"Is that pizza for us?" Wiggles hopped onto his hind legs and waggled his front paws in the air.

Tate nodded. "It wouldn't be right to ignore my two best customers." He flipped open the lid of the box and pulled out a delicious slice of three cheese and garlic sauce pizza and gave it to Wiggles.

Wiggles made short work of the slice and was begging for a second piece within seconds.

I took my own slice and continued to watch as the crew unloaded the truck. "I'm trying to figure out if our visitors really believe in shifters and magic. From what I've seen of this crew, none of them have any powers, unless they're hiding it."

Tate's expression tightened, making his handsome face look sharp. "I've heard of the guy who's running this show. His name's Kirk Wrangler."

I glanced up at Tate. "That name's familiar."

"It should be. The guy's famous for claiming to have hunted down dozens of supernatural creatures, mainly shifters. It was only a matter of time before he sniffed out this place and came poking around."

My eyebrows lifted at the harshness in Tate's tone. For a werewolf, he was one of the most relaxed guys I'd ever met. "This sounds personal."

Tate lifted one shoulder. "Kirk nearly caught a friend of mine. Hundreds of people turned up to track him down. The guy's a bit of an idiot and went on a rampage one night. He left so much evidence behind, even a nonbeliever would have had a hard time arguing there was no such thing as werewolves. They tracked him for two weeks without letting up. He was so exhausted by the end, he was about ready to throw up his paws and give up. I got him out just before they shot him, but it was a close call. Kirk's ruthless. This is all about making a big name for himself and a heap of cash while he's doing it."

"So this Kirk guy must have magic if he can locate shifters."

"Not that I know of," Tate said. "I've kept an eye on him over the years. He thinks shifters should be locked in zoos, so we can be studied to find a way to eliminate the threat."

"Do you think he wants to wipe out magic?" I already didn't like Kirk for invading our beautiful village, and he'd just plummeted in my estimations if he was eliminating shifters.

"Witches and hellhounds are probably safe." He shot me a smile. "But maybe that's because Kirk doesn't know you exist. I reckon he sees shifters like big game. It's an ego thing about wanting to hunt down something more powerful than he is. It makes me sick. I can't believe the mayor let this guy set up in Willow Tree Falls."

"Mannie always wants to put this place on the map, but even I'm surprised he's letting this happen." I chewed on my slice of pizza as several cars rumbled past, none of their engines sounding happy. Mechanical vehicles never did well in the village because the magic short-circuited them. I'd seen a dozen cars break down.

"I don't like this." Tate crossed his arms over his broad chest and flexed his large biceps.

"You'll be fine. You never cause any problems when you shift."

"That you know of." He winked at me, some of the old Tate charm returning.

"We should monitor the shifters in the village," I said. "We don't want anyone coming to the attention of Kirk, just in case he really is here to find a new trophy for his wall."

Tate shuddered. "I've already put the word out. Most of the shifters know Kirk by his lousy reputation. Some of our older residents aren't that strong, though. They could need extra support to stay hidden. I wish Kirk had never come here. Our old timers just want a quiet life. That's why they moved here."

On the outside, Willow Tree Falls was just another sleepy village, but I'd lived here all my life. Scratch the surface, and there were all kinds of magical deeds going on. It was one of the reasons I loved this place so much.

"There you are!" Dazielle rushed toward me, her large angel wings fluttering around her. "I've just been to Cloven Hoof. I couldn't find you."

"The club doesn't open for hours," I said. "What's up?"

Dazielle stabbed a finger at the truck being unloaded.

"We were wondering why you'd let a shifter hunter set up in the village," I said. "Did you and Mannie get a big payoff to look the other way while he hunts our innocent shifters?"

Dazielle's plump cheeks flushed. "Of course not. I can't be corrupted with a bribe. I wouldn't be heading up Angel Force if I could. But..."

"But what?" I said.

She sighed. "Kirk Wrangler tricked Mannie and me."

"You can be tricked?" The angel who headed up law enforcement in the village wasn't always top of the class when it came to not being duped. Angels were pretty but often not that smart.

A scowl marred Dazielle's face. "I had several conversations with Mr. Wrangler. He assured me he'd be bringing an entertainment and information show, something fun to entice more tourists. And Mannie always welcomes the opportunity to have tourists visit us."

"More like our mayor welcomes their money," I said. "We have enough tourists. We don't need more."

"But this is out of season. The tourists only visit when the weather is warm. No one wants to look at our stone circle in the middle of winter when it's snowing."

"Good. That means the people who live here get some quiet time."

Dazielle waved a hand in the air. "Mr. Wrangler said he'd bring a show of curiosities. He's a collector of magical artifacts. I was fascinated by the proposal and wanted to see what he'd collected."

"He probably stole those artifacts from our ancestors," I said.

"If I find anything of my ancestors in his possession, I'm taking it back," Tate grumbled.

Dazielle narrowed her eyes at him. "Don't do anything foolish."

"It won't be foolish. It's my right to take back something this moron stole from a shifter."

I looked on with interest as they squared up to each other. I wouldn't mind seeing Tate go up against Dazielle. They were both supernaturally strong and fast.

"Does Kirk have magic of his own?" I asked Dazielle.

She tore her gaze from Tate. "No, we met after I'd arranged his permits. He's not magical."

I groaned. "This just gets worse. You gave him a permit to hunt us?"

"No! I knew nothing about the hunting equipment being unloaded from the trucks. We didn't agree to that. I gave him a permit for a curiosity exhibition, show, and guided walks."

"Guided walks that include silver cages and weapons."

"You've seen weapons?" Dazielle's face paled.

"Not yet, but it's only a matter of time."

"I've been trying to get his permit revoked, but Kirk has three lawyers working for him, and they're proving difficult and threatening to sue. There's nothing I can do to stop this from happening."

"Dazielle! It looks like Kirk's going shifter hunting. He could kill someone. Let him sue you. He can't do this."

"He won't." Tate's voice was a low grumble as his werewolf side peeked out. "If that guy lays a finger on any of the shifters, he'll have me to answer to."

"No! I don't want vigilante justice going on here," Dazielle said. "My angels are monitoring the situation."

"I feel so much better for knowing that," I said. "We should run Kirk out of the village."

Tate passed Wiggles another slice of pizza. "I'm happy to lead that project. He can take his nasty silver cage and get lost. If I have to apply my boot to his backside to make it happen, that's fine by me."

"No attacking him. Kirk's done nothing wrong," Dazielle said.

"Yet," I muttered. "If we give him enough time, he could cause serious problems."

"I have things under control." Dazielle frowned as boxes were carried up the hill toward the huge marquee being set up.

"How about the angels monitor Kirk and we keep an eye on the shifters?" I said to her. We had an uneasy alliance when it came to law enforcement. Dazielle had grown to tolerate my interference, as she called it, in her cases, especially since I'd gotten good at solving murders. And I just about tolerated being around a self-righteous angel, who shed feathers everywhere and ordered me about as if she owned me.

"That's why I was looking for you," Dazielle said. "Kirk has a big crew working for him, and I need some extra muscle."

"I always knew you enjoyed having me around," I said.

"I want to be involved too," Tate said. "I've got plenty of muscle, and the shifters trust me. They'll listen if I tell them to keep a low profile while Kirk and his goons are in the village."

"What about the pizza?" Wiggles said. "You can't shut down Mystic Mushroom."

Tate chuckled. "You think pizza is more important than keeping our shifters safe?"

Wiggles' furry forehead wrinkled. "If I say yes, does that make me a bad hellhound?"

Tate petted him on the head. "Don't worry about the pizza. There'll be plenty to go around."

Wiggles wagged his tail. "So long as you don't forget us hungry hellhounds, I'm up for a little creep monitoring."

"I overheard some of Kirk's crew joking about werewolves," I said. "That's their focus. Although all shifters will need a warning about him."

Tate growled again. "I'd love to know where he's getting his information."

"Stories crop up all the time about big cat sightings, yetis, and animals with glowing eyes out on the moors, but we've always kept those stories quiet so we don't attract idiots with weapons." I pursed my lips as I looked at Dazielle. "And we never give them permits to visit and shoot us."

Dazielle sighed. "I never said Kirk could shoot anything. I am trying to fix things."

"Try harder," I said.

"Most of the shifters around here keep their heads down and their noses clean," Tate said. "It wouldn't have been any of them causing a stir and getting noticed. Although some of the older guys can be eccentric."

"When you say eccentric, you mean they frequently get arrested for running around with no clothes on and baying at the moon," Dazielle said.

"We all get our kicks where we can," I said. "If that's the worst our resident shifters do, you should be grateful."

"I had toothless Brian in a cell for two days because he refused to put on any pants," Dazielle said. "That's not a sight any of us need to see."

I wrinkled my nose. Toothless Brian was a harmless, ancient werewolf with no teeth and blunt claws. He liked to hang around the thermal spa and scare tourists for kicks. Ancient werewolves often got quirky. When you've been around for a few hundred years regularly shifting into a werewolf, it tampers with your sanity and, seemingly, makes you forget about wearing pants.

"We'll team up," I said to Tate. "We'll handle the shifters. Dazielle and the rest of the angels can keep an eye on Kirk and his crew."

"That's fine by me," Tate said.

"I give the orders when it comes to law enforcement," Dazielle said.

I crossed my arms over my chest. "So, what are your orders?"

She looked over at the truck as more boxes were unloaded. "I'll handle Kirk. Now he's gotten what he wants, he's not being so friendly. I tried to speak to him when he arrived, but he brushed me off and passed me to his harassed assistant. He's not the nicest man to deal with, and I don't want you getting in trouble if he ruffles your feathers." She glanced at me.

I shrugged. I knew what trouble she was talking about. I was still having the occasional problem with my demon, Frank. He was as strong and annoying as ever, and neither of us liked dealing with jerks. It brought out our mean sides.

Tate cracked his knuckles. "If Kirk tries anything—"

"You tell me about it," Dazielle said. "I don't want to spend the next year dealing with lawyers because that... that poop head found a loophole in my permit."

I snorted a laugh. That was the strongest cuss word I'd ever heard Dazielle say. She must be angry. "Let's get rid of him while we can. I'll hex him, Tate can go all super wolf on him, and..." I gestured at Wiggles to include him in this plan.

He licked his muzzle clean of pizza crumbs. "I'll gas him with my unique hellhound aroma."

Dazielle shook her head. "We're doing this properly. We'll monitor the situation and see what Kirk has planned."

"And if he goes hunting shifters?" I said.

"We'll make sure he doesn't catch them," Tate said, "by any means necessary."

"No, not by any means necessary," Dazielle said.

I squeezed Tate's arm. "We'll make sure the shifters are safe and Kirk doesn't get his grubby little hands on them."

Tate heaved out a sigh then nodded.

I was glad to have a project to focus on. Aurora was away on another vacation with her new husband, Lex, I hadn't had a demon hunting job for weeks, and I still hadn't figured out my problems with my boyfriend, if he was still that. This was just the distraction I needed to ignore my messy personal life.

"I'll try to speak to Kirk again," Dazielle said. "Figure out what he's planning."

"I can talk to the shifters," Tate said. "I'll make sure they know to keep a low profile until this idiot has left."

"Keep me informed." Dazielle nodded at us before striding toward the trucks.

"It's a good idea to chat to your shifter buddies," I said, "but I also think we should talk to Kirk."

"Dazielle won't like that," Tate said.

I arched an eyebrow at him. "Are you scared of the angels?"

He chuckled. "Kind of. Dazielle would kick my butt in a fight."

"I was wondering about that. An angel against a werewolf. You don't think you can take her?"

"I'd have a go, but it's not so much her wings that bother me. She gets to see the health and safety reports on the store. Dazielle could make my life difficult if I get on the wrong side of her. She could even shut down Mystic Mushroom."

Wiggles groaned. "Whatever you do, don't annoy Dazielle. Your pizza is the best. I'd be miserable if you got shut down."

"We won't annoy her. Besides, she can't get angry if she doesn't know what we're doing," I said. "Dazielle plays by the rules, and it sounds like Kirk doesn't. If that's the case, I'm happy to bend them to make sure he sees sense and moves on quickly."

"That works for me. What do you want to do first?" Tate said.

"We'll deal with the shifters while Dazielle does what she needs to do with Kirk, then we'll have a friendly chat with him to make sure he doesn't tear Willow Tree Falls apart in his shifter hunt or learn too much about our perfect little town and its unique residents."

It was time to go find our shifters.

Chapter 2

I tipped back my seat and stretched my arms over my head. It was quiet inside Mystic Mushroom, the late-afternoon lull before the after-work crowd appeared, desperate for Tate's delicious pizza.

Wiggles burped quietly under the table and rested his chin on my foot. He'd been sneaking pizza all afternoon, along with a fair few dough balls, and now resembled one, his gut ballooning out as he snoozed.

We'd spent hours sending messages on the snow globe network and even meeting a few shifters to let them know Kirk was in the village and that they didn't want to be anywhere near him. Most were happy to oblige, but a few were angry and wanted to stand up to Kirk. They were the ones that had me worried.

If Kirk wasn't careful, he'd have a bunch of miffed shifters deciding they wanted to turn the tables and hunt him down.

I wouldn't mind being a part of that group. Kirk Wrangler gave me the chills. I hated it when non-magic users invaded our sacred space and tried to make out there was something wrong with us.

Magic had been a part of the world since it began, but those who didn't have it feared it or envied it, and that often led to them trying to destroy it.

Tate appeared from the kitchen, wiping his hands on a clean cloth. His T-shirt sleeves were pushed up almost to his shoulders, revealing black swirling tattoos around his muscles. "Okay, everything's prepped for the evening rush. I've got half an hour to spare."

"Then let's go introduce ourselves to Kirk," I said.

Tate removed the apron from around his waist. "From what Dazielle said about him, he's not a guy to be easily swayed."

"Then he's not met us." I stood from my seat, disturbing Wiggles from his carb-induced slumber.

He rolled over and shook himself. "Is it time for more pizza?"

"No. You've eaten way too much. You'll make yourself sick."

Wiggles burped again. "I feel like I've eaten too much cheese. I've got a gone off milk taste on my tongue."

"Then definitely no more pizza for you," I said.

"That's cruelty to animals," he said. "You can't deprive me of my pizza."

Tate locked the store, and we walked along the main street in the village. "There's plenty more pizza. But you have eaten three large stuffed crusts today and two side orders of dough balls."

"Whoa! I didn't know you'd had that much," I said. "No wonder you're almost rolling along the street."

"I can never resist Tate's gooey deliciousness," Wiggles said.

Tate roared a laugh. "That's the biggest compliment I've ever had."

We walked along quietly for a moment.

"I spoke to Rhett recently," Tate said.

I slid him a glance, trying to ignore my stomach doing a weird flip. "I'm happy for you."

"He asked about you."

I stuffed my hands into my jeans pockets and looked at the ground. Things hadn't been right between Rhett and me ever since a member of his gang got accused of murder. I'd been investigating the case, and things had gotten difficult between us. Rhett had accused me of being more angel than witch.

"I take it you're still not talking?" Tate said.

"You got it. Until he apologizes, nothing's changed. Besides, he's not even around. He left the village without telling me where he was going." I was smarting over his lack of contact. Anyone would think he was trying to forget about me. Maybe he already had.

"Rhett figured it was for the best," Tate said. "He was finding it hard to keep bumping into you."

"Sure he was," I said. "Not that I care what he does. Rhett made it clear he doesn't want to be in my life."

"Tempest, that's not true. Rhett's always had a thing for you. Long before you got together."

"Maybe he had a thing for me," I said. "People change."

"He's a stubborn guy and can be proud. And he's fiercely protective of his gang. Cut him some slack."

"I do. All the time. But he put them before me. And he lied to me. That's hard to get over."

Tate nodded as we headed up the hill toward the stone circle where Kirk and his crew were setting up a marquee. "Haven't you ever made a mistake?"

I glared at him. "Sure, we all mess up. But we're supposed to be on the same side. He acted like I was the enemy."

Tate lifted his hands. "I get it. I hope you work things out. You're like the power couple of Willow Tree Falls. It's weird not seeing you together."

I snorted a laugh. "How about we focus on this power hungry idiot and leave my love life out of it?"

"Whatever you say. I just wanted you to know Rhett still likes you, but he's not sure how to figure things out."

"A gift subscription to a brownie delivery service would go a long way," Wiggles said. "You can't go wrong with a regular delivery of sweet treats."

I smiled at Wiggles and shook my head. The trouble was, I didn't know how to fix things either. I had a tendency to hold a grudge, and Rhett had hurt me by lying. Maybe it was easier to go back to the single life.

My heart didn't like that idea and gave a hard thump at the thought of letting go of Rhett for good.

Tate slowed as we approached the large green marquee. "Is that a wolf pelt?" He pointed at the glass cabinet being wheeled inside.

I caught hold of his elbow and gave it a squeeze. "Keep calm. If Kirk's got his whole collection here, there could be some gross things inside."

Tate growled, sounding remarkably like a wolf. "He's exhibiting his kills. How is that something to be proud of? This guy needs to be taught a lesson."

"Not here," I said. "If this is too much for you to handle, I can deal with Kirk on my own."

Tate's eyes glowed amber before he shook his head and rolled his shoulders. "I've got this, and I need to know what he's all about. Maybe he's more dangerous than I realized."

"He won't skin any shifters while he's here," I said.

"If he does, I'll return the favor on his pale hide," Tate grumbled low in his chest.

"Have you got your wolf under control? We're not moving until I'm sure you're not going to wolf out on me."

Tate's nostrils flared. "I'll be fine. Let's get this over with."

We marched into the marquee. On one side was a long row of wooden benches. The rest of the space had been set up like a museum exhibit. There were display cabinets, large glass-fronted cases with shelves, and numerous display boards.

I walked to the nearest cabinet and looked inside. I sucked in a breath, and my stomach rolled over. "He's got mummified witch parts in here."

Tate joined me and looked in the cabinet. "Are they real?"

I pressed my hand against the glass, focusing on a skull that was supposed to have been from a witch who'd killed a thousand people with her dark magic. "It's so old that it's hard to tell. I'm picking up a faint charge of magic, but these body parts could have come from anywhere. They're probably fakes." I hoped they were fakes. Seeing the bones of a witch on display only made my mood darken.

"The exhibition isn't yet open to the public."

I turned at the sound of the deep, smooth voice behind us. A guy in his mid-forties wearing a tailored black suit and a white shirt open at the collar stood in front of me. He had slicked-back dark hair with traces of silver through it.

His dark gaze ran over me, and he smiled. "I'm Kirk Wrangler. Welcome to my exhibition. You must be eager to see the delights on offer if you snuck in without being spotted."

I ignored his outstretched hand. "Tempest Crypt. This is Tate Rathmore. We live in Willow Tree Falls."

"What are you doing with all this stuff?" Tate jabbed a finger at the wolf pelt.

Kirk's eyes narrowed a fraction. "Don't tell me you're an animal rights campaigner? I've had trouble from them in the past."

"I don't believe in skinning an animal and then using it to make money," Tate said.

"That pelt came from a deadly creature, hell-bent on killing anyone who stumbled into its path." Kirk leaned closer. "The legend goes that it was controlled by a dark magic user. They filled the wolf with evil spells and sent it on a rampage as revenge on a slighted love."

I snorted my disbelief. "It looks like a common wolf pelt to me."

"There was nothing common about it when it was full of magic. If you visit the displays when the event is open, you'll learn all about it then." Kirk gestured to the exit.

We didn't move.

He sighed. "Perhaps you could educate me about your home. Are you both... attuned to the unique nature of the village?"

"You've lost me," I said. Was this guy prodding to see if we'd reveal our magic?

Kirk spread out his hands. "I've heard fascinating rumors about this place. And I hear some residents have unique abilities. What skills do you have, Tempest?"

I rolled my eyes at the lecherous look on his face. "None that you'll ever get to see. What's your exhibition about?"

Kirk flicked his gaze to Tate. "Entertainment and education. It opens the minds of everyone who visits, so they see the true wonders of the world. All its magic and secrets."

"You're telling me these really are the body parts of witches?" I jerked my thumb at the case full of mummified remains.

"Why not? Don't tell me you aren't a believer in magic."

"What I don't believe in is exploitation," I said. "If these are fake, then you're lying to people. And I don't imagine this'll be free to visit."

"People are always happy to pay to be entertained. And it's important I cover my costs. My charge is small for such an adventure." Kirk pointed at the exit again. "Now, I must ask you both to leave. You don't want to spoil any of my surprises."

"What about the hunting party?" Tate's hands clenched, and a muscle in his jaw ticked.

"Hunting party?" There was a momentary flash of surprise on Kirk's face before he tipped back on his heels.

"We heard you're looking for a special creature," I said.

"One that has a pelt like that." Tate pointed to the wolf skin.

"Hunting wolves isn't legal around here," Kirk said. "And I never break the law or lie."

"Not even to get a permit from our mayor?" My top lip curled back.

Kirk shrugged. "You'd have to speak to my assistant about permits. That's admin work. But you'd be wise not to be so closed-minded about magic. Many people believe that artifacts such as that wolf pelt are real and came from a creature that has no place in our world. We'd no sooner let a madman run loose on the streets than let a dangerous, flesh-eating beast remain on the loose."

"What kind of beast are you talking about?" I said.

"A thing that shouldn't be allowed to roam. An evil thing." Kirk theatrically whispered the last two words and twirled a hand in the air.

"And you plan to put a stop to these evil things?"

"I see no harm in doing so. I have years of experience dealing with the unexplainable phenomena of this world."

"What makes you qualified to do that?" I said.

Wiggles nudged my leg with his head.

Kirk glanced at Wiggles and did a double-take. "His eyes are a strange color."

"He's got pink eye," I said. "It's contagious. You don't want to get too close."

Kirk continued to stare at Wiggles. "They look like they're glowing."

I was surprised he could see Wiggles' red eyes. Maybe he had some magic about him. "It's a trick of the light."

Wiggles shuffled back and ducked his head.

I glanced at Tate. Most people with no magic filtered out the unusual and unexplainable. They wouldn't see Dazielle's enormous wings. They'd just see a stunning blonde dressed in white. But now and again, you met someone who could see past the filters. And it looked like Kirk was one such person. Bad luck for us.

"Don't worry about my dog," I said. "But we're here to give you some advice while you're staying in Willow Tree Falls."

Wiggles continued to head-butt my leg.

"Advice I didn't ask for," Kirk said.

"But you need to listen to it." I leaned closer, allowing a shimmer of magic to flare behind my eyes. "Take care while you're in our village."

Kirk smirked. "Why would that be? I'm not doing any harm. Perhaps this sleepy village needs shaking up."

"It doesn't. It's a special place."

"I can sense that." Kirk rubbed his hands together. "I have a good feeling. Things will change once I've spent time here. This could be the making of me."

"Or the end of you," Tate muttered.

"We don't like outsiders causing trouble," I said. "People move here for the peace. They don't like to be bothered by tricksters."

"I'm a trickster? That's not very welcoming."

"I'm not trying to be welcoming," I said.

"You'll have no trouble from me, so long as I find nothing... concerning," Kirk said.

Tate stepped forward and glared at Kirk. "Leave. You're not wanted here."

"Oh! Mr. Wrangler. I'm sorry to interrupt, but I need you to take a look at this inventory." A pretty Elven woman with long, shiny black hair and brilliant blue eyes dashed over.

"Not now, Sabine." Kirk waved his hand at her.

Stress radiated off her in unwelcome waves. "There's... something missing. I've looked everywhere for it."

Kirk turned and glared at Sabine until she looked away and took a step back. "I'm busy. Get another member of the team to help you find whatever is missing. It can't be that important."

"I've had people searching." Sabine glanced at us with large eyes. "It's the amulet case. There are a dozen amulets missing. You always tell me how powerful they are and that we need to be careful with them."

Kirk's hand shot to his mouth, and he pressed a finger against his lips. "Not now. I'm dealing with some residents. You blabbing about missing items won't reassure them of our professional operation."

"I already know what kind of shady business you're running," Tate said.

"Amulets?" I said. "Are these amulets supposed to have magic in them?"

Kirk glared at Sabine for several more seconds before turning back to me. "They're rare and interesting objects. Perhaps you'd like to look at them. Oh, that won't be possible, since my soon to be fired assistant has lost them."

Sabine squeaked and backed away. "I didn't lose them. I can't—"

"Find them or find yourself a new job."

"I've looked everywhere," Sabine mumbled. "I wanted to check you hadn't moved them or decided not to use them for this event."

"They're always a part of the exhibition. They must be somewhere. Look again. And keep looking until you locate them."

"You never know, they could have magicked themselves away," I said.

"Or the werewolf you're planning on hunting took them," Tate said.

Sabine's eyes grew even wider. "They... they know about that?"

"Stop talking," Kirk said, "or you really will find yourself out of a job."

Wiggles head-butted my leg again.

I glanced down at him. He was panting, and that wasn't like him. I bent and pretended to adjust his collar.

"What's up?" I whispered.

He hopped his paws onto my knee so his mouth was by my ear. "I feel terrible."

"It's your own fault for eating so much food. Give me five minutes with this idiot, then we'll go outside. You'll feel better in the fresh air."

"This place does stink. There's definitely magic in here."

I petted him on the head and then stood. "We'd like to look around before we go. That won't be a problem, will it?"

Kirk shook his head. "That won't be possible. I've got my permit and the okay from the mayor for my work to go ahead. You can come in with everyone else when the place is ready. It wouldn't be fair to give you a sneak preview. Besides, I'm behind schedule. I haven't long gotten rid of the local law enforcement, and they spent a long time checking over everything. In fact, they were almost as suspicious as you."

"That's because we work together. They use my skills on a freelance basis." Perhaps dropping my angel bomb association would get Kirk to be more cooperative.

He didn't appear to be impressed. "In what capacity? You don't look like a police officer."

"And you don't look like someone I can trust."

"Sabine! There you are." A tall blonde with a big smile dashed over and wrapped her arms around Sabine. "We've been looking for you everywhere, and it took ages to find this little place. There were no signposts, so we kept getting turned around. Anyone would think the villagers don't want tourists coming in."

The tension leached out of Sabine as she hugged the woman. "Bella! I can't believe you made it. Did you come alone? Where's Oakley?"

"The car broke down the second we got into the village. It's like we passed a barrier that said no cars allowed and the engine gave up. He's got his head under the hood. He'll be here soon." Bella stepped back and looked around the marquee. "Wow! This is something else. When you said you were coming here with a magic exhibition, we just had to visit."

"Any idea who she is?" I whispered to Tate.

"Nope. She's not from around here. Must live nearby."

Kirk loudly cleared his throat. "Sabine is working."

"Oh! I'm sorry. I won't get in the way." Bella smiled at Kirk. "But I couldn't let my best friend pass by without a visit. We don't live far away, and I had to see all the magical things she's always telling me about."

Sabine grinned. "Prepare to be amazed. This stuff is incredible."

Kirk's gaze ran over Bella. "Perhaps I can give you a private tour, Miss...?"

"Rossi. Bella Rossi." She shook Kirk's hand. "That's sweet of you. Oakley can come along, too."

Kirk's smarmy smile faded. "Your husband?"

Bella giggled. "Noooo! Another friend. He'll be here soon."

Wiggles stumbled over to Kirk, gave a loud burp, and then puked on his shiny shoes.

I pressed my lips together and tried not to laugh as Kirk leaped away, cursing and flicking his feet around. "These are imported leather! They're ruined."

"He didn't mean to puke on you," I said. Although Wiggles had definitely been working hard to get his aim right.

"Gah! No animals in the exhibition. Get him out of here." Kirk stamped away, muttering to himself.

"Nice work, Wiggles. That guy was also making me feel queasy," Tate said.

Wiggles burped.

"Could you take him outside for me?" I said to Tate. "I want to look around while Kirk's out of the way."

"Sure thing. My pizza probably had a role in that explosion, so I'll keep an eye on him," Tate said.

"Your pizza is fine. It's the quantity Wiggles ate that's the problem." I shook my head at Wiggles and gave him a stroke. "Plain chicken and rice diet for you for a few days."

He snorted at me and stomped out of the marquee with Tate.

Sabine looked down at the pile of puke Wiggles had left behind. It was a grossly impressive amount for such a small dog. She sighed. "I'm gonna have to clean that up."

"Sorry. He ate something that didn't agree with him. He kept trying to tell me he didn't feel so good, but I was focused on Kirk. He seems like an interesting guy. What's he like as a boss?"

Sabine bit her bottom lip. "Um... He's okay."

"Don't you dare be nice about him. He's horrible," Bella said. "I don't know why Sabine stays in this job."

"I love the artifacts," Sabine said. "You know that. Besides, I can't get any other work with only a history degree and no practical experience. It was this or work in the local café. Kirk is difficult, but so long as I keep out of his way, I get to look at loads of interesting things."

"Including a missing box of amulets?" I said.

Sabine shook her head, her face paling. "I don't know where they've gone. I was certain they were on the back of the last truck, but it's been unloaded, and they're not there. Bella, can you help me look for them? Kirk will be busy fussing over his shoes, so I've still got time to salvage this and keep my job."

"No problem. I'll help you hunt them."

"Hey, I thought I'd never find you." A tall, broad shouldered guy with shaggy blond hair that gave him a surfer vibe walked over to us.

Sabine's cheeks flushed, and she smiled. "Hey, Oakley. Thanks for bringing Bella here to see me."

He bent and kissed her cheek, affection shining in his eyes. "Any time. And I wanted to see you, too." He stared down at Sabine for several seconds, and neither of them spoke.

"What do you think of this place?" Sabine was the first to look away.

Oakley's gaze cut around the marquee. "It looks good. Although I got talking to a couple of guys who helped me push the car to safety, and they said there's a hunt being planned. I thought this was all about the occult."

"A hunt?" Bella tipped her head. "What are they hunting in a place like this? It's not as if there are bears or lions roaming the countryside. Maybe a few overfed cats."

I arched an eyebrow. There were plenty of dangerous things lurking out there, but I wasn't going to mention them to Bella. She looked like she'd scare easily.

"Kirk's been stirring up trouble. He's convinced there's a wild animal out there." Sabine glanced at me. "Your friend mentioned werewolves."

I nodded, watching her closely to see how she reacted to that idea. "You get all sorts in our woods."

Bella laughed. "There are no such thing as werewolves."

Oakley glanced out the marquee. "If there is, it's almost a full moon. Good hunting conditions."

Bella thumped him good naturedly. "Come off it. You can't believe in that." She looked at Sabine. "Tell me this isn't true."

Sabine gestured around her. "Kirk believes in all kinds of weird things."

"So long as it makes him money," I said.

She shrugged. "He never misses an opportunity to make money. But I shouldn't say any more about it, or Kirk will only get madder, and he's already angry because of the amulets. He'll dock my wages if I can't find them."

"We'll find your missing trinkets," Bella said. "Go on. Tell us more about this hunt."

Sabine sighed. "Kirk is telling people that a werewolf has been spotted in the area."

Bella and Oakley laughed. I remained silent.

"Your boss is an idiot. I've always thought that. And I can't believe you're still working for him," Oakley said.

"I like this job." Sabine's forehead wrinkled. "Besides, I'm a free agent now. I can do what I like."

That comment wiped the easy smile off Oakley's face. There was definitely a relationship vibe going on between them, although they didn't seem to be acting particularly like a couple.

"People must know it's a joke," Bella said. "I bet it's some poor wild dog gone rabid."

"No. We look after all the animals around here," I said.

"Maybe it's a wolf," Bella said. "In some places, conservation projects are letting wolves back into the wild."

"And beavers," Oakley said. "Beavers are worse than wolves."

"How do you figure that?" Sabine said. "Have you been savaged by many angry beavers?"

"No, but I wouldn't want to get bitten by one. And they clog up the rivers, dry out fertile land, and cause damage to ancient woodlands. They may look cute, but beavers are the things you need to look out for."

"We have no dangerous beavers around here either," I said. "Kirk's wasting his time getting people whipped up with his stories."

"He's made a lot of money selling advance tickets to the hunting party. It's an exclusive event," Sabine said.

My stomach clenched. How did Kirk even know that werewolves roamed the village?

"That's what I heard outside," Oakley said. "Everyone's excited about it, and someone was showing off a gun. They reckoned it contained silver bullets."

This was going from bad to worse. Things would get out of control if a group of ill-informed non-magic users started firing at anything that looked remotely wild, especially since that description accounted for half the population of Willow Tree Falls.

This had to stop. This was my sanctuary and my home. If Kirk laid a finger on any of our resident werewolves, he'd have to answer to me. Maybe I'd skin him and mount him. We could display him at the entrance to Willow Tree Falls as a warning to anyone dumb enough to try something like this again.

"Come with me. I need your help to look for these amulets," Sabine said to Bella and Oakley. She glanced at me. "And you'd better go. If Kirk sees you're still here, he'll only get mean."

Although I wasn't scared of Kirk, I did need to leave. I wanted to check on Wiggles and then make sure our shifters were safe. Some were bound to ignore the advice we'd given them to keep their furry heads down.

I dashed out of the marquee and over to Tate and Wiggles. "We have a big problem. Kirk's been selling tickets to groups of hunters. And they want a werewolf."

Wiggles and Tate growled at the same time.

"I knew it," Tate said.

"I didn't like the smell of that guy the second I met him," Wiggles said.

"He's got so much testosterone running through him that it aggravated my wolf. This is just a massive ego trip for him," Tate said.

"We're here to deflate that ego." I looked down at Wiggles. "How are you feeling?"

"Hungry. Although I'm no longer in the mood for pizza. I could handle some doughnuts though."

"You're having plain chicken and rice for the next twenty-four hours," I said, "or you'll be hurling your guts up again."

"That sounds dull," Wiggles said. "Can I have cheeseburgers to go with that?"

"No cheeseburgers," I said.

"We need to make sure Kirk leaves before he causes trouble," Tate said.

"I agree," Wiggles said. "Although he'll probably have concession stalls. I wonder if I can get a cheeseburger from the marquee."

"No more rich food! I left Sabine to clean up your mess. That's not fair on her since she already has to deal with Kirk."

"Although your aim was perfect, Wiggles," Tate said.

Wiggles wriggled his furry butt. "I was attempting to puke in style."

"Enough talk about gross things. We need to focus on the unpleasant task of dealing with Kirk."

"What can we do to keep him from messing with our shifters?" Tate said.

"We arrange our own hunting party to keep our shifters safe. We hunt the hunters and make sure they don't cause problems," I said.

"You want to take down some humans?" Wiggles cocked his head.

"Not for good, but some may need some gentle incapacitation to make sure they do no harm."

"We don't have much time left to figure this out," Tate said. "The sun's going down."

"Then let's move." I turned and slammed into someone. I grabbed their shoulders to stop from tumbling to the ground. When I flung my hair out of my eyes, I came face-to-face with Zandra.

Chapter 3

"What are you doing here?" I released my hold on Zandra and stepped back. My half-sister looked eerily like me, with the same pale skin and dark hair. She was also ten years older than she was supposed to be.

She clutched a large box in her hands, tight to her chest. "I'm working."

"You're working for Kirk Wrangler?" My top lip curled. "You're joking?"

"Who's this?" Tate said. "We've not met before."

Zandra shrugged. "I'm no one."

I opened my mouth then shut it. Zandra's history wasn't an easy topic to unpick. After my dad lost his memory and walked away from the family, he started a new life, and Zandra was the result. Now she was in Willow Tree Falls, and after trying to jinx my other sister, Aurora, and almost ruining her wedding day, things weren't easy between us.

"You must have a name," Tate said. "I've not seen you in Mystic Mushroom. Are you new to the village, or do you just not like pizza?"

Zandra shook her head. "You ask a lot of questions. Are you always this nosy?"

"Tate's being friendly," I said. "Tate Rathmore, this is Zandra."

"Hey, Zandra. Do you need a hand with that box?" Tate said.

"Nope. I can manage on my own." Zandra didn't return Tate's warm smile.

"Tate, you go ahead. I need a word with Zandra." I still wasn't sure how to introduce her to people. There were only a few others who knew we were related, and I wasn't sure if Zandra wanted our connection shouted around the village. Gossip spread like wildfire around here. And Dad didn't yet know she'd cast a spell on herself to grow up so quickly.

"I'll make sure any stubborn shifters get a reminder to stay away from the woods tonight to avoid the hunters." Tate nodded at Zandra then dashed away.

"What's going on?" Zandra said. "What's up with the shifters?"

"Your new boss is interested in hunting down a werewolf."

"Huh! He said nothing about that when I was hired. He kept on about showing the world magic was real. He gave me the creeps."

"He is a creep, and he's after our shifters. He's not a nice guy."

"Kirk may not be nice, but he's paying me. It's tricky finding work around here without revealing who I am," Zandra said.

"And who are you?" Wiggles said.

Zandra stared at me. "Um..."

"You smell familiar. We've not met before, but I know you've been around the village. You smell like a Crypt witch," Wiggles said.

"Um..." Zandra lifted one shoulder and widened her eyes at me.

It wasn't my secret to tell, but it couldn't be fun for Zandra that people didn't know who she was. It was partly her fault for being so elusive, but Dad should have been handling this, and he'd dropped the ball.

"Wiggles, I'll tell you who Zandra is, but you need to keep quiet about it," I said.

"Yeah, you don't want the family secret getting out and embarrassing anyone," Zandra said.

"I didn't mean it like that," I said. "But Mom and Dad are still working it out. I don't want to make things harder on them."

"Sure, I know. You have to look after your own."

Gah! Zandra could be a brat. Even though she looked eighteen, she still acted like an eight-year-old.

"Who is she?" Wiggles said.

I sucked in a breath. "Wiggles, this is Zandra. She's my half-sister."

He tilted his head from side to side, looking at us in turn. "Oh! It makes sense now. You have a similar vibe, and you kind of look the same. This happened while your dad was absent without leave and lost his memory?"

"Yup," I said. "And Zandra cast a spell to grow up fast. She shouldn't be this age."

Zandra bristled, her lower lip jutting out. "Says who?"

"The laws of magic. And nature."

"Cool! Okay, I'm going to check out the trash around the back of the marquee for leftovers." He trotted away, not fazed by the news.

"Will I get a talking dog if I join the family?" Zandra said. "I wouldn't mind my own hellhound. That one's small, though. Aren't they usually bigger?"

I turned back to face her. "Wiggles is unique. He used to be a regular dog. Then someone hit him with their car. Aurora and I brought him back. When he opened his eyes, he was different."

"Whoa! You brought him back from the dead?" Zandra's eyes flashed. "Resurrection magic is difficult. You mess up one tiny thing and you end up with a brain dead, shambling flesh eater who'll destroy you."

"It sounds like you've tried that kind of magic, too."

"Not yet. But I want to."

"Don't. Crypt witches know how to handle powerful magic," I said. "But we also know about being careful with power. And I've experienced your magic. It's strong."

"Yeah, you have, so you'd better be careful around me." Zandra grinned.

She may find it amusing, but Zandra was wielding powerful magic, and I wasn't certain she could control it.

"Does Dad know you're working here?" I said.

Zandra adjusted her grip on the box, and her grin faded. "He doesn't. I mean, it's none of his business. I haven't seen him since the whole age spell took effect."

"It needs to be his business if you're sticking around."

Zandra had been in the village when Aurora was getting married to Lex but left soon afterward. I hadn't expected to see her again, so it was a shock to find her working for Mr. Sleaze. Not a bad shock, but I was getting used to having another sister.

"I wasn't planning on coming back, but I got word that this exhibition was setting up in the village, and I was curious. Plus, I'm allowed to be here. After all, most of my family live here."

"Of course you can be here. We want you here."

"Most of the family know nothing about me."

"That's not true. They'd all like to meet you."

"Yeah? Well maybe I don't want to see them. And I've been busy," she said.

"Working for scumbags like Kirk Wrangler. Are you that desperate for money?"

"My finances are none of your business." She glanced over her shoulder. "Although he is a real jerk. He's yelled at me twice. I've got an idea though, a way to speed this thing up and still get paid for my full hours. I'm helping set up the exhibition in one of the smaller tents. Follow me." Zandra strode away, and I had no choice but to follow if I wanted to keep the conversation going.

"Do you think Kirk has magic?" I asked.

"Not that I've picked up on, but he loves to be the boss. He yells and stamps his feet like a spoiled child if he doesn't get his own way."

"What did he hire you to do?"

"Fetching and carrying and setting up a few of the displays. It's cash in hand and easy work. It's just for the week while the exhibition is here. I knew nothing about him chasing after shifters."

"I reckon Kirk uses these exhibitions as a cover. It gets him in places of interest, so he can look for shifters. Although I have no clue how he knows they're real." I entered the tent behind Zandra and walked to a display cabinet. There were tribal masks and a few strings of beaded jewelry inside. There was nothing magical about them.

A shiver of magic pulsed over me, and I turned. My heart leaped into my throat.

Zandra had her arms outstretched, pulses of green magic firing from her. There were fragile glass ornaments dancing through the air and heading toward an empty cabinet.

My spine shuddered at the intensity of my half-sister's magic. She had so much power, but it felt unstable, as if it might burst out of her at any second.

Although Zandra hadn't told me much about her upbringing, she hadn't had much training in how to use her magic when she was young.

"Maybe you shouldn't—"

"Shush. I'm concentrating." Zandra's eyes narrowed as more items danced out of the box.

I ducked as a spell caster made of bones and feathers shot past my head. "Your magic is agitated."

"I know what I'm doing." Zandra spoke through gritted teeth.

I squeaked as an axe head skimmed past my forehead, almost scalping me. I shot out a spell, weaving it through Zandra's, grabbing as many objects as I could.

"Hey! Stop interfering. I can do this."

"You don't have to prove anything to me. I know you can do strong magic. Set the artifacts down. We'll put them in the cases by hand."

"Get lost." Zandra shoved her hands out, and another wave of spiky, unstable magic filled the air.

The objects swirled around us, but rather than heading to the display cabinets, they spun in a spiral, up to the top of the tent.

"That was your fault," Zandra said. "I was controlling them until you added your magic."

"Draw in your spell slowly. The objects should come down without breaking. The spell you cast is twisted. It's confused and doesn't know what you want it to do."

"I don't need your help."

Wiggles wandered into the tent, chewing on something he'd most likely gotten out of the trash. He was smacked on the side of the head by a spinning bowl. He growled and belched smoke before racing over to me, dodging flying objects.

"What's going on?"

"Zandra's showing off her magic," I muttered.

"I'm not showing off. I've almost got this. Get out of my face with your stupid spell."

I shrugged and drew back my magic, keeping it poised on the tips of my fingers just in case.

The objects wavered in the air and continued to spin to the top of the tent and remain there.

Wiggles swallowed whatever he was chewing. "It's getting busy out there. People are taking this shifter hunt seriously."

That's what I needed to focus on. Not Zandra and her anger issues. I shot out another spell, grabbed the spinning artifacts, and propelled them toward the display cabinet.

I was almost done, when I was jerked off my feet and landed flat on my back.

Zandra glared at me, one finger pointed in my direction and another at the objects. "Keep out of my business, big sister."

I jumped to my feet. "What's the matter with you? I'm helping."

"You're interfering."

"I'm trying to stop you from making a mistake." I jammed my hands on my hips, ducking at the last second as the axe head spun past me again.

Zandra shot me another glare and thrust a second wave of magic across the tent.

"We should make a run for it while we're both conscious," Wiggles said.

The objects danced precariously in the air then slammed together, shards of pottery, glass, and bone raining down on us.

I ducked and covered Wiggles as the air was filled with sharp shards of debris. There was a popping sound and then silence.

I looked up to see Zandra's cheeks were bright red and her lips pressed together.

A quick glance around the tent showed none of the objects had survived her magic.

I stood and brushed shards of bone and pottery from my hair and shook off my jacket. "I'm guessing this wasn't what Kirk wanted you to do."

Zandra grunted. "He was an idiot, anyway. None of these things are important. There wasn't a hint of magic in them. And it's your fault they broke."

"Sure it was. How about we get out of here before Kirk sees this mess and fires you?"

Zandra shrugged. "I've got nothing else to do. And he paid me half upfront, so at least I earned something."

"How about you help me with our shifter problem?" Zandra was a hothead, but we were related, and I knew only too well how it felt to not be in control of your magic.

Her eyes sparkled. "Sure. That's more interesting than this. What have the shifters been up to?"

"The shifters aren't the problem. It's the idiots hunting them we need to deal with."

Several hours after Zandra's spectacular smashing of an entire collection of ancient artifacts, we were outside, walking as quietly as possible through the gloom, under the canopy of the Willow Tree Falls woods.

Tate and Wiggles were also with us, and we were looking for shifters who hadn't heard the message to keep their heads down while the hunting parties were about.

A large, almost full moon hung over our heads, which made it trickier for the shifters. A full moon brought out their wild sides, and some of them had little control when the moon ordered their primal urges to do a little howling, a little growling, and a lot of scaring.

"I hear three groups over to my left," Tate said, his werewolf hearing coming in handy. "There must be at least fifty people on the hunt."

"There are more in front of us," Wiggles said. "I keep hearing them blundering around."

"They'll be lucky not to get killed," I said. "Fallon will be furious about so many people traipsing around in her beloved woods." As forest guardian, Fallon took her role seriously. She had deadly traps set up for anyone foolish enough to blunder around when she didn't want them there.

"I see torchlight behind us," Zandra said. "At least two groups."

"We're surrounded by morons," I said. "I can't understand why this many people would want to hurt a lovely old werewolf."

"Maybe it's the vicious fangs giving them the shivers," Wiggles said, "or the fact they might get eaten."

Wiggles wasn't a huge fan of werewolves, Tate aside. He'd had a rumble with one many moons ago and gotten his furry behind whipped.

"Most of our werewolves have no interest in eating people," Tate said. "It's too much hassle. Now, if we're talking a nice succulent deer, that's a different story."

"They fear what they don't understand," Zandra said. "It's the same with our magic. They don't understand it, they can't have it, so they don't like it. They want it gone."

I nodded. We had a museum of witchcraft and magic in the village that showed our long and often unhappy history of associating with non-magicals. The outcome for magic users was usually a violent one and ended with lives being lost.

"We need to run diversions," Tate said.

"Good idea. We can lead the groups away from the woods, so they don't stumble over something furry that doesn't want to be disturbed," I said.

"They shouldn't find any shifters in here, but you know what some of the old ones are like. They're stubborn and forgetful," Tate said. "I'm fast on my feet, so I'll go make some noise, add in a few creepy howls, and lead them out of here."

"I'll do the same," Wiggles said. "I'm feeling much lighter after barfing up that pizza. And I can do an awesome howl. I'll even throw in some stinky smoke to get them excited."

"We'll stay in the middle of the woods and monitor any hunters who linger behind," I said. "I haven't seen Kirk yet, and I want to watch out for him."

Tate and Wiggles headed off, leaving me with Zandra.

We walked along together without speaking for a while, stopping occasionally to follow the groups still in the woods.

There were several loud, eerie howls, followed by excited shouts as the groups chased after Wiggles and Tate.

"That should keep them busy for the night," I said.

Zandra nodded and kept walking.

I still wasn't certain how to handle her. We were family, but I'd only gotten to know about her, and she wasn't the easiest person to connect with. Plus, she'd almost ruined Aurora and Lex's wedding by kidnapping the groom. It hadn't been the perfect introduction to the family.

But I wanted her to stick around. Not being able to control your magic was scary, especially when you were dealing with it on your own. I knew all about difficult magic, having lived with a troublemaking demon lodged inside me ever since I was a kid. It made me different, and I often felt on the edge of things. Not pure witch, not all demon. I was a bit of a magical conundrum.

I nudged Zandra with my elbow. "If you need help with your magic, I know a few things."

"Like you could help me," Zandra said.

I sighed. Shut down with a single sentence. "It's just an idea. I am older than you."

"You're going to pull the big sister card on me?" Zandra shook her head. "Does that work with Aurora?"

"Not often. Usually, she ignores everything I tell her."

Zandra huffed out a laugh. "I can't imagine your perfect sister ever causing you trouble."

"Aurora has her moments. She was once under the influence of a warlock who convinced her to marry him. He turned her into a Stepford wife and then a stone dragon when his dirty deed was discovered."

Zandra's jaw dropped. "You're kidding? How did you get her back?"

I tilted my head from side to side. With some sacrifice on my part. I'd do anything for my awesome family. "It's amazing what you can do when you know how to control your magic."

Zandra kicked a stone along the ground. "Maybe I could do with pointers. Even when I try the simple stuff, it's always more powerful than I want it to be. I never meant to age ten years, but I tested the spell, and wham! I'm almost twenty. My magic has a mind of its own. Is that something you can control?"

"Sure. Everyone's the same when they first gain their abilities. It took me ages to master fire magic. Now, I can toss out a fireball with the best of them."

"Sounds good. But... it's not just magic I need help with," Zandra said.

"What else is going on? Guy trouble?"

"As if." She glanced at me. "I need a job. I have no qualifications since I never finished school. I didn't want to take that job working for Kirk, but I was desperate. Not many people want to hire me. I was told I was acerbic."

"I'm stunned. You seem to make friends with everyone you meet."

"Sure I do. It always feels like the nice parts of my personality got given to Aurora. When Dad talks about her, he tells me how amazing she is."

I was about to protest but stopped. I used to feel I was living under Aurora's sparkly white shadow. She was the perfect witch. Plus, she was beautiful, funny, ran a successful business, was sweet to everyone, and had recently gotten her happily ever after with a ridiculously wealthy genie who lived in an enormous castle.

"Aurora's not perfect," I said.

"You're telling me you don't like her?"

"I like her fine. I love her. She's my sister. But she can be naïve. She's terrible at making decisions, and she has a really sweet tooth. She's worse than Frank when it comes to sugar."

Zandra's gaze ran over me. "Your demon likes cake?"

"It's one of the few things that'll keep him quiet. A huge sugar overdose will placate him for a while."

"I didn't know that about demons. I've not met many. I keep out of their way."

"It's a good thing to do. Most are junk food fiends, but Frank is on a different level. Whenever I let him out, we end the night breaking into a candy store or a bakery, and he gorges himself on sweet treats. Then I have to spend the next week burning off the extra calories. Although I always run hot when Frank's in control, so that helps to burn through the sugar."

Zandra laughed. "That has to be a joke."

"No joke. You'd think he'd want to end his freedom by going on a violent rampage, and he's come close, but I can always sway him. I need to make sure I have the details of some expensive patisserie in my pocket, and Frank always heads there. He goes out on a sugar high. Once he's content, I can get back control."

"I'll remember that if your demon ever causes me trouble," Zandra said.

"He will if you stick around long enough," I said. "And you should stay around. How about you try working with me at Cloven Hoof?"

Her eyes widened. "You want me to work for you?"

"I do. Two of my staff have gone off for a three-month trip around the world, so I'm shorthanded. Have you got experience in bar work?"

Her shoulders dropped. "No. I mean... I'm eight, going on eighteen."

"Oh! Sure. That's not a problem. You can learn."

"Are you sure you want me there? I'm not good with people."

"I do. It'll be good for both of us. We can get to know each other, work on your magic control, and I can train you to have better people skills." Although mine weren't exactly stellar, but I kept things friendly in the bar and the regulars coming back, so I was doing something right.

"Thanks. A job would be good." Zandra's smile looked tentative, but at least it was there.

"Great. Swing by the club tomorrow at five. I'll get you started."

A high-pitched, female scream ricocheted through the trees, making us freeze.

Zandra grabbed my arm. "That sounded bad."

Another scream rang out.

"That sounded human. Let's go. Someone's in trouble."

We raced through the trees, my heart pounding. We broke through into a clearing, and I pulled up short.

A woman was on the ground, her long dark hair partially covering her face, and her hands covered in blood.

Chapter 4

I raced over and caught hold of the woman's shoulder. "What happened?"

She shied away from me, her whole body shaking. "There was this... Giant ape. It came out of nowhere. It lunged and tried to eat me."

Zandra joined me and stared down at the woman, disbelief on her face. "There aren't apes in these woods."

I glanced at her and raised my eyebrows. Maybe there weren't any primates, but there were plenty of other creatures that would take a bite out of someone if they weren't paying attention.

"There is! It bit me. I thought I'd die. I kept screaming and must have scared it off. It had me in a tight embrace and was sucking my blood."

I knelt beside her. "What's your name?"

"Roxanne." She blinked big tear-filled eyes at me. She was pretty, with dark eyes, a full mouth, and lots of dark curly hair. "The bite really hurts."

"I'm Tempest. I live around here. Let me look and see how bad it is." I also wanted to check out the type of bite mark. Were we dealing with a rogue vampire?

Roxanne winced as she moved her hand away from the wound.

I grimaced at the clear row of teeth marks. "It must be painful, but it doesn't look too deep."

"What if I've been bitten by a rabid animal?" Roxanne groaned. "I don't feel so good. What are the symptoms of rabies?"

"Stupidity?" Zandra muttered.

"Can you stand?" I said to Roxanne.

"I think so." She twisted her long dark hair around one hand.

"Let's get you up. You'll feel better when you're not sitting in the dirt." I gestured for Zandra to help, and between the two of us, we got Roxanne on her feet.

She wobbled from side to side but remained standing.

"Can you describe this creature to me?" I said.

"I already said, some kind of murderous ape. It was at least seven foot tall, with dark shaggy hair all over its body, and long limbs. And it had evil little eyes. I think it was lying in wait for someone to eat," Roxanne said. "It lunged out of the trees and came straight for me."

"What are you doing in the woods at this time of night?" I said.

"I'm here with my boyfriend. He's excited about the exhibition in the village. He reckons he's going to see a werewolf. It's all rubbish, but he told me it would be fun and promised me we'd go to dinner after he'd wasted a few hours looking around for this creature. But then I got turned around in the woods and lost him. That's when the creature attacked."

"It's this way! I heard the scream come from over here."

I turned at the sound of Cassiel's voice and looked at Zandra. "You may want to disappear. Our local law enforcement is about to arrive."

Zandra's mouth twisted to the side before she nodded. "Good idea. I'll see you tomorrow." She glanced around at the trees before slinking away just before the angels appeared.

Cassiel appeared through the tree line, accompanied by Dazielle.

Dazielle strode over, her expression tight. "What happened here?"

"I was attacked." Roxanne blinked up at the angels. "I almost died."

"The bite's not that serious," I said. "You won't even need stitches."

"It feels serious to me," Roxanne said. "You shouldn't have creatures like that roaming these woods. It's not safe."

"Says the woman chasing a giant wolf in the middle of the night," I muttered.

"Let's get you looked at," Dazielle said. "Cassiel is our medical expert. We'll get you to the hospital if you need to go."

Cassiel led Roxanne away and settled her on a nearby tree stump before inspecting her neck wound.

"What's going on out here?" Dazielle snapped at me.

"Roxanne over there reckons some big ape attacked her. She's probably been drinking."

"You should be controlling this situation," Dazielle said. "You're in charge of monitoring shifter activity, while I keep watch over Kirk."

"I am monitoring it. And none of our shifters are stupid enough to wander around the woods tonight biting people. How's Kirk behaving himself?"

"He's eating dinner."

"He's not out hunting with everyone else?"

"Not yet. But we have a problem. This is the second bite victim we've had tonight," Dazielle said. "Someone didn't get the message about not eating the tourists."

"Is the other bite victim okay?"

"She's scared and talking about some big bear stalking her, but she'll be fine."

I glanced at Roxanne. "It does sound like something's attacking the tourists. Something that shouldn't be out here."

"And something you should have warned to stay away if you were doing your job properly."

"A job you're not paying me for. And I don't control the shifters. Maybe it's not a local. Someone could have come for a fun weekend and ended up being hunted. It could have spooked them and they attacked."

"Whatever it is, it has to stop before things get out of hand. Kirk has already heard about the first attack. He's stirring up trouble by telling people there's a dangerous creature on the loose that needs to be eliminated."

My hands flexed. "He'd better not touch our shifters."

Dazielle looked over at Cassiel. "How are things going over there?"

Cassiel raised a hand. "Everything's good. I've cleaned the wound. It's not a deep bite. She'll be fine."

Roxanne looked up at Cassiel and fluttered her long lashes. "You're my heroine. Thank you so much for rescuing me."

I arched an eyebrow. Hadn't I been the one to rescue her?

"Let's get you back to the station," Dazielle said to Roxanne. "We'd like to take your statement if you're up to it."

"Of course. Anything I can do to help. You need to catch this beast before someone is killed." Roxanne clasped Cassiel's arm and clung on tight.

I followed along behind them as we headed out of the woods. I wanted to find out more about the first bite victim. Two attacks in one night wasn't a coincidence. Tate and Wiggles could hold things down in the woods and keep the hunters distracted while I learned more.

We walked into Angel Force and through to the back office. Cassiel took Roxanne to an interview room to get her statement, while I remained with Dazielle.

"Have you got pictures of the first victim's wounds?" I said. "I got a good look at Roxanne's wound, so I should be able to tell if it's the same creature that attacked them both."

"Give me a minute." Dazielle strode off and returned with a file. "The woman's already left, but we got her statement and photographs."

I flipped open the file and had a look. There was a row of neat, flat bite marks on the side of her neck.

"We can rule out a vampire," I said.

"Agreed. There are no puncture marks on either victim."

"These don't look like the bite marks from any creature with fangs. They look like the mark a human would leave behind."

"Or a witch."

I arched a brow at her. "Same goes for an angel. Where are all your angels tonight? Off biting tourists for fun?"

Dazielle tutted. "It's none of my angels."

"And it's none of the witches." I placed the photos back in the file. "Is another tourist attacking people?"

"Why would they do that?"

I shrugged. "I never understand what motivates non-magicals."

Dazielle turned as the door into the office slammed open. Tate staggered through with a woman in his arms, Wiggles trotting along beside him.

I rushed over with Dazielle. "What happened to her?"

Tate looked down at the woman, who was clinging to him and crying. "I was out with Wiggles, chasing off... I mean, taking him for a walk, when we heard Lucy calling for help." He tried to put the woman down, but she clung on and sobbed louder.

Tate lifted one shoulder. "She got attacked by something in the woods."

"Another one," Dazielle muttered. "This is all we need."

"You're safe now," Tate said to Lucy. "The police will help you. Let me put you down."

"No, don't leave me. You saved me. I'm only safe with you," she said.

I bit my bottom lip to stop from smiling. Any woman would feel safe in Tate's arms. He was gorgeous, strong, and served the best pizza in the village. But if she knew what he turned into when his blood lust was up, she wouldn't be so clingy.

"Bring Lucy this way," Dazielle said. "We'll find someone to look after you, miss. You're safe. Nothing can get you in here."

I waited with Wiggles as Tate carried the sobbing Lucy away with Dazielle. "Are you seeing a pattern here?"

"Nope. I'm only seeing a distinct lack of food," Wiggles said. "I worked up a huge appetite diverting those hunting parties. I've been racing around the woods for ages."

"You've been doing it for less than an hour. You can't be that hungry."

"I'm famished. Did you forget I lost that amazing pizza all over that guy's shoes?"

My gaze flicked back to the file, and I read through the first victim's information again. She was twenty-five, slim, with long dark hair. She had a bite on the right side of her neck, just like the other victims.

Dazielle strode back to us. "This has to stop. I can't have some wild creature, human or not, running around the woods biting people. I'm not sure how we will cover this up. There are too many tourists in the area, so the news will leak out."

"We can wipe their memories before they leave," I said. "And none of the bite marks are deep. They probably won't even leave a scar. There'll be no evidence this ever happened."

"That's hardly the point. I'm worried. Whoever is doing this could be working up the courage to kill," Dazielle said.

"If they are, then they have a type they want dead." I held the file out. "All the victims are young, attractive women who look the same. Slim, pretty, with long dark hair. We've got a serial biter on our hands."

Dazielle scowled at me. "Wait here. I need to get a team together to send out and put a stop to this." She marched away again.

I headed over to make myself a coffee and hunted out a cookie for Wiggles.

"How did you get on diverting the parties in the woods?" I said to him.

"They were easy to fool. I kept racing around and making weird noises. They got excited and chased after me. If they got too close, I hid under a bush until they passed."

"What's the mood like out there?" I took a sip of my coffee.

"Not great." Tate strode over, running a hand through his hair. "The visitors want blood, and they want it soon."

"How's Lucy doing?" I said.

"She's shaken up. She keeps saying some big shaggy bear chased her."

"That's the third bite victim tonight," I said. "I found someone in the woods, and she described her attacker as a giant, hairy ape."

"There are no shifters around here like that," Tate said. "It can't be a local guy."

"But something is out there biting people," I said. "It has to be a magic using creature, because we don't have bears or apes in the woods. We need to get back out there along with the angels to track this biter down before he kills someone."

"We do," Tate said. "And the groups are getting mean. As I was bringing Lucy in, I heard someone say Kirk has put out a reward to capture the creature, dead or alive."

I groaned. "That's the last thing we need. People are already stirred up. Throw in a money incentive, and it'll be carnage out there."

Dominic raced in, his wing feathers ruffled and a streak of blood down one wing.

"Dominic, are you hurt?" I hurried over to him.

"No, I'm fine. But I'm glad you're here, Tempest. You need to come with me." He grabbed my arm.

"Why? What's going on?"

"It's your Uncle Kenny. He's in trouble. A mob has got him cornered. They think he's been attacking people. If we don't hurry, they could kill him."

Chapter 5

I choked out a laugh. "This is a joke. Uncle Kenny doesn't even kill spiders."

"No joke. Hurry! We don't have much time." Dominic tugged me toward the door.

My heart plunged to my boots and flew back to my chest. Dominic looked terrified. He wasn't messing about.

"Tate, stay here and see if you can find out any useful information from the women who've been bitten." I was already running to the door with Dominic and Wiggles.

"Sure. You don't want me to come with you?"

"No, you're good. I've got this." I was still reeling from the shock of Dominic's news as we dashed outside. "Where's Uncle Kenny?"

"On the other side of the woods," Dominic said. "It's a trek on foot, but I can get us there quickly if we fly."

"Let's do it." I scooped up Wiggles and clutched him to my chest. Dominic had flown me around a few times before, but it was a sensation that took a while to get used to, like the first drop on a rollercoaster.

Dominic wrapped his arms around my waist, and we shot into the air.

Wiggles let out a whoop and pedaled his legs. "This is what being an angel feels like. I need to get myself a pair of wings."

I clutched him tightly as we soared toward the forest. "Dominic, tell me what happened with Uncle Kenny."

"I was out doing a patrol of the woods, when I heard raised voices. I went to investigate and discovered twenty people surrounding someone. I couldn't believe it when I saw your Uncle Kenny was being hassled."

"Why do they think he's been attacking people?" Uncle Kenny was the most peaceful guy I'd ever met. He was quiet, sweet, and thoughtful. He complemented my auntie Queenie's loudness perfectly.

Dominic's hold on me tightened a fraction. "He looked disheveled. And he had blood on his hands."

"Blood! Whose blood? Was it his? Did someone attack him?" Heat rose up my neck, and a trickle of Frank's energy stirred inside me.

"No, but I couldn't get close enough to see what was going on. The crowd had him penned in and they were yelling, saying he'd attacked those women."

"He'd never do that. You do know that?"

"I know Kenny well. He's a good guy."

"Why didn't you stop them from hassling him?"

"I tried to, but there were too many."

"They're human. They're easy to stop."

"Not without revealing my magic, which would have complicated things. And there were no other angels around, so I raced back to find you." Dominic swooped low over the trees and headed toward the ground. "That's the crowd up ahead. We'd better go the last bit on foot, so they don't see me flying in."

I squinted, and my gut clenched as I saw Uncle Kenny with his back against a tree. He had his hands out as if trying to placate the surrounding mob.

"Fly us in behind Uncle Kenny," I said.

Dominic swooped around, and we dropped among the trees. The second he let me go, I was off and running with Wiggles.

My heart was pounding and my stomach tight. No one threatened a member of my family and got away with it.

I emerged beside the tree where Uncle Kenny was trapped.

He shot a fear-filled glance my way, then a breath rushed out of him. "Tempest! I'm glad to see you. Things are getting tense around here."

I looked down at his hands and grimaced. They were covered in blood. "What's going on? Are you injured?"

"He's a killer!" someone in the crowd yelled.

"No, he's not," I snapped. "Why have you got this man hemmed in?"

Dominic emerged on the other side of the tree, a tense expression on his face.

"Arrest that man," someone shouted.

Wiggles grumbled a bark, sounding remarkably like a regular dog as he glared at the angry crowd.

Dominic looked at Uncle Kenny. "Why do they want you arrested?"

"I was trying to help someone I found in the woods." Uncle Kenny gestured behind him.

"You weren't helping her. You'd just killed her and got caught before you could run off," another shout came from the crowd. "Bring out the body for the police to see."

My eyes widened. "There's a body?"

Uncle Kenny nodded, his face pale. "They won't listen to me. I was in the woods and discovered a woman who'd been attacked. I was seeing if she was still alive when this crowd appeared. They surrounded me, pulled me away from the body, and started yelling."

"If there's a body, it shouldn't be moved," I said. "You'll destroy evidence. Show me where she is."

"It's too late for that," Dominic muttered.

I turned to see two people carrying a woman's body between them. They set her down in front of Uncle Kenny and backed away.

I gasped. "I know her. She worked for Kirk Wrangler at the magic exhibition. That's Sabine."

"And that monster you're protecting murdered her." One of the guys who'd carried out the body jabbed a finger at Uncle Kenny.

Wiggles gave another warning grumble.

I knelt beside Sabine. Just like the other victims, there was a large bite mark on the right side of her neck, but there was a lot more blood and dirt on her clothing as if she'd fallen and scrambled through the mud. She could have put up a fight, which would mean her attacker would also be muddy and covered in blood.

I glanced at Uncle Kenny's hands and mud-stained pants. His appearance didn't exactly make him look innocent.

"Where was she found?" I said.

"Just back there in the woods," Uncle Kenny said. "That's where I discovered her."

"That's where you killed her," the other man who'd brought out Sabine said. "You have to pay for what you've done."

Dominic stood in front of Uncle Kenny, his posture upright. "We don't know this man had anything to do with this woman's death. We'll question him, but we need to examine the scene and figure out what happened."

I stood and joined Dominic. "Everyone needs to leave. If this is a crime scene, you're damaging evidence by being here."

"We don't need any more evidence. It's clear what happened. This maniac attacked this innocent woman and savaged her to death." The guy who seemed in charge of this group loomed in front of me. He had an angry gleam in his pale blue eyes, and his face was pink and sweaty.

"I didn't do this," Uncle Kenny whispered to me. "You know I'd never hurt anyone."

"You don't need to convince me," I said. "Everyone calm down and go home. This isn't helping."

"We're not leaving until we have justice," the man said. "And if you won't deal with him, we will. Hand him over."

"You're not touching him," I said. "Leave now."

"Are you going to make us?" The guy pushed into my personal space and peered down at me.

Wiggles barked again.

I refused to be intimidated by the guy and met his glare head on.

Dominic yelped as three people barged into him and took him to the ground. They rolled away in a blur of fists.

"Step aside, or you'll be next," the guy in front of me said. "If you're protecting a killer, you deserve everything you get."

I didn't enjoy using magic on humans. It was difficult to know how they'd respond to a spell. Some took it well, while others had a magic hangover for days. But I couldn't save this idiot's feelings. He wanted Uncle Kenny's blood, and he wasn't going to get it.

"Back off. This is your final warning." I let a little of Frank's energy through. People always got skittish when a demon was looming nearby.

The guy took a step back, his gaze narrowing. "The police in this village have no idea what they're doing. If you let him loose, more women will be murdered. We have to stop him now. Why are you protecting a killer?"

"I'm protecting an innocent man." I clasped my hands behind my back and conjured a lightning spell.

Uncle Kenny squeezed my hand, adding his own magic to supercharge the spell.

There was a growl of thunder over our heads, which made several people look up and murmur.

"Stay down, Wiggles. It's going to get crazy in a few seconds," I said.

Just as the guy in front of me lunged, a huge bolt of lightning slammed into the ground. He yelled and lurched away, while the rest of the crowd scattered.

The strong chlorine-like smell of ozone hung in the air as I blinked my eyes, dazzled by the intense blast that had smashed a few feet away from me.

The guy who'd been about to attack was flat on his back, blinking up at the sky. "Huh! There's not supposed to be any storms tonight."

I blasted down another bolt of lightning. It cracked into the ground between the guy's legs and sent any stragglers fleeing.

"Get out of the woods, everyone," the guy yelled as he staggered to his feet and did a quick inspection of his groin to check he hadn't lost anything important. "The trees are attracting the lightning. It's not safe in here." His gaze cut to Uncle Kenny.

"Don't even think about it," I said. "We'll deal with him."

He muttered under his breath as he raced away.

Uncle Kenny sighed as I turned to him and gave him a hug. "Thanks, Tempest. I thought I was done for."

I stepped back and ran my gaze over him. He was pale, bruised, and bloody. "Is that your blood?"

Uncle Kenny looked down at his hands and shook his head. "It's the victim's blood. She was a mess when I found her."

There was a rush of cold air over our heads, and I looked up to see Dazielle descending.

"I figured that lightning must have had something to do with you." She landed lightly on her feet and strode over. She looked down at the body on the ground and then at the huge scorch marks from the lightning blasts. Her shoulders tightened.

"Before you jump to conclusions, Uncle Kenny didn't kill this woman," I said.

"According to the crowd racing out of the woods, he did," Dazielle said. "Kenny, I need to take you in for questioning."

"I was only trying to help her," he said. "I found her in the woods like this."

"Why are you covered in her blood?" Dazielle said.

"He's not covered in anything. He's just got some on his hands and on his shirt," I said.

"Which is enough to worry me," Dazielle said.

"You sound as bad as the mob we just scared away. They think he killed Sabine," I said.

"Sabine?"

"That's the dead woman's name. I met her at the marquee. She worked for Kirk Wrangler."

Dazielle nodded. "I didn't think I recognized her. Why are you in the woods at this time of night, Kenny? You must have known there'd be trouble tonight."

I also wouldn't mind hearing the answer to that question. Uncle Kenny liked early nights with a mug of cocoa and a good book, and it was odd to find him out so late, but I didn't want him to say anything that might implicate him. Once Dazielle got an idea in her head about a suspect, it was almost impossible to shake it loose.

"Don't interrogate Uncle Kenny now," I said. "He's in shock. He was almost attacked by that mob of idiots. And they moved the body. They destroyed evidence."

"How convenient for Kenny," Dazielle said.

I glowered at her. "He didn't do this."

"He still has to come in for questioning," Dazielle said.

Dominic staggered into view, his wings muddy and a streak of dirt down one cheek.

"What happened to you?" Dazielle said.

"I told you, we had a baying mob around us that wanted trouble," I said.

Dominic nodded as he brushed down his clothes. "They were angry. I was protecting Kenny when three of them jumped me."

Uncle Kenny placed a hand on my shoulder and squeezed. "It's okay. I'll go with Dazielle and get this sorted out."

I turned and hugged him. "I know you didn't do this."

"Let's go to Angel Force," Dazielle said. "Dominic, stay with the body. I'll send Cassiel to look over the scene before we move Sabine."

Dominic glanced around the dark woods, before pulling back his shoulders and nodding. "Of course. I'll stay."

I caught hold of Uncle Kenny's elbow and held on tightly as we walked back to Angel Force. I'd find a way to show he was innocent, even if I had to interrogate every irritating tourist who was polluting our wonderful village.

There was no way he was guilty of murder.

Chapter 6

We were back at Angel Force and waiting in an interview room. I was becoming such a regular here, I'd have to put in a request for my own desk and a dog bed for Wiggles.

Uncle Kenny sat at a table, while I paced the room and Wiggles snored in the corner.

"They should at least have let you clean yourself up," I said.

Uncle Kenny frowned at his grubby hands. "I wouldn't mind getting this blood off me, and I really might kill for a strong cup of coffee. I'm exhausted."

"I can fix that. Denying a person his caffeine is a crime. Wiggles, wait here with Uncle Kenny."

Wiggles lifted his head, nodded, and then closed his eyes.

I headed out of the interview room and made two coffees. After the shock of finding Uncle Kenny at a murder scene, I could also do with a hit of caffeine.

It wouldn't be long before word got around that he was in trouble. I should warn the rest of the family what was going on, but hopefully, we could get everything cleared up and I could get him home before the rumors reached them.

I was heading back to the interview room when Dazielle appeared.

"I hope this won't take long. It's getting late, and I should be out there keeping an eye on the angry mob," I said.

Dazielle glanced my way. "Your lightning magic scared off most of them. You shouldn't use magic in front of humans."

"They had no clue it was me. How long will this take?"

"It won't take long at all if Kenny confesses."

"He'll never confess, because he didn't do it."

"Let's go see if that's true." Dazielle plucked a coffee from my hand. "I'm assuming you want to sit in on the interview."

"You have no choice but to let me in there."

She arched an eyebrow but made no comment as she headed into the interview room.

I was right behind her and passed Uncle Kenny his coffee.

"Thanks, Tempest." He took a sip and then nodded at Dazielle. "I know it doesn't look great for me, but I had nothing to do with that woman's death."

Dazielle settled in the seat opposite Uncle Kenny. "Let's start at the beginning. What time did you find the body?"

"Around midnight."

"How did you find her?" Dazielle said.

"I was in the woods, walking around."

"Why were you in the woods so late?" I said.

His gaze cut to me and he shifted in his seat. "I was interested in what was going on. I heard about the hunting parties."

"You wanted to join in?" Dazielle said.

"He'd never do that," I said. "Uncle Kenny's a pacifist."

A small smile crossed his face. "I don't like violence. That's very true. I was out walking around, making sure no one was at risk of the hunting parties, when I heard a noise."

"What kind of noise?" Dazielle said.

"A sort of shuffling sound and a small groan. I thought one of our visitors had had an accident in the woods. It's easy to do in the dark, and we all know Fallon likes to leave traps everywhere. I was worried someone had gotten in trouble."

"That's when you found Sabine?" I said.

Dazielle glared at me.

"That's right. And I think I saw the killer," he said.

"Who was it?" I said.

"I don't know. I didn't get a good look. I had my flashlight pointed at my feet so I could see where I was going. When I heard the noises, I flashed it around a few times and saw a large figure leaning down. They got startled and ran off the second the beam of my flashlight touched them. They were large but fast."

"You can't give me any more details about this individual?" Dazielle said.

Uncle Kenny glanced my way and took a sip of coffee. "They were tall."

"That's it?"

"Sorry, it was dark. I stumbled over to see what they were interested in. That's when I found the woman, Sabine."

"Was the victim dead when you found her?" Dazielle said.

"She was. Only by a couple of minutes, if that." He swallowed. "She was still warm, and blood was leaking out of her neck. I tried to stop it, which is how I came to have it on my hands, but I was too late."

"The blood came from the bite mark on her neck?" I said. "That's just like the other victims—"

"That's enough, Tempest." Dazielle glared at me. "Perhaps Kenny also knows about those victims, so we don't want to give him too much information."

"Come off it. You can't think he's the one biting people," I said.

Uncle Kenny blinked several times. "Other people have been killed tonight?"

"Not killed," I said. "But other women have been bitten on the neck tonight. Only Sabine died."

Uncle Kenny raised a shaking hand to his mouth but grimaced when he saw the dried blood on it and placed it back on the table. "I had no idea."

"Was there anyone else with you in the woods?" Dazielle said. "Anyone who can corroborate what you've told me?"

There was a slamming noise from outside the interview room and several yells.

The door was shoved open, and Auntie Queenie appeared. Uh oh! Word sure traveled fast in this village.

Her cheeks were flushed, and she was holding a handful of white feathers, which she dropped on the floor.

"Queenie, you can't be here. This is a closed interview," Dazielle said.

Auntie Queenie ignored her and rushed to Uncle Kenny. She threw her arms around him and hugged him. "What's going on? Why do the angels have you? I've heard all kinds of horrible stories."

"Your husband is being questioned as a suspect in a murder," Dazielle said.

Auntie Queenie gasped. "You really have lost your senses this time, Dazielle. You know Kenny. He'd never do anything like that." She stroked a hand across his hair, smoothing it down. "Let's get out of here."

"He's not going anywhere," Dazielle said. "I'm still questioning him. I may keep him here overnight."

The worry in Auntie Queenie's eyes made my heart clench as she caught my gaze. "You shouldn't have let the angels bring him here, Tempest."

"It's fine," Uncle Kenny said. "I want to help. And I did discover the victim in the woods."

"And now you're being interrogated by the angels for helping." Auntie Queenie shook her head. "You're wasting your time, Dazielle. I was with Kenny all night."

I pursed my lips. That didn't sound right. Auntie Queenie wasn't one for traipsing around the woods in the middle of the night. Neither of them were.

"If you were with him all night, where were you when I found him?" Dazielle said.

Auntie Queenie lifted her chin. "I got caught short and had to find somewhere to go without being watched. The woods are full of idiots tonight, so it took me a while to find somewhere where I wouldn't be disturbed."

"I think I saw the killer. I scared him off," Uncle Kenny said.

"Which we only have your word for," Dazielle said.

"And mine," Auntie Queenie said. "I was with him. I was gone for maybe ten minutes. Kenny couldn't have done any harm in that time. Not that he ever would. And you'd know that if you had your head screwed on right."

"Auntie Queenie, are you sure about this?" She was giving Uncle Kenny a false alibi. It could get them both in trouble.

Her expression became defiant. "I'm certain. I know where I was."

Dazielle sighed and shook her head. "Kenny would have had an opportunity to commit the murder while you were... Spending a penny."

"He didn't," Auntie Queenie said. "I'm his alibi. And there's no reason for him to go stalking women in the woods. He has all the woman he needs in me."

Uncle Kenny chuckled and patted her hand. "You bet I do."

"Is there anything you'd like to add, Kenny?" Dazielle said. "You're willing to let your wife be your alibi?"

Auntie Queenie squeezed his shoulder and lifted her eyebrows at him.

He let out a soft sigh. "I know better than to question my wife."

I frowned. She was lying, and that only made me more worried. Uncle Kenny was innocent, I was certain of it, but why did Auntie Queenie feel the need to cover for him? Did she know something I didn't?

"Well, I won't get any more useful information tonight," Dazielle said. "Not now you've got your big guns out protecting you, Kenny."

"And it's late," Auntie Queenie said. "It's wrong to question people when they're tired and out of sorts. Kenny's in shock. And why didn't you let him get himself cleaned up? I can smell all that muck on his hands. It's turning my stomach."

"We needed scrapings from under his nails. He can wash up now." Dazielle stood and pushed back her chair. "I will want to speak to you again, Kenny. On your own next time."

"Of course. I want to clear my name," he said.

"That's enough," Auntie Queenie said. "Home to bed with you. Let's move, Tempest."

I gave Dazielle a shrug as we raced out of the interview room and left Angel Force. Everyone knew better than to stop the determined force of Auntie Queenie when she was on a mission.

"I'm sorry about this," Uncle Kenny said. "I never meant to get any of you involved."

"Hush. Don't talk such nonsense. If you need help, we'll be involved." Auntie Queenie stroked a hand down Uncle Kenny's back as we hurried along.

The streets were almost empty. The late hour had driven most of the crowds away.

"Let's get inside," Auntie Queenie said. "Everyone could use a large stiff drink after this unpleasant adventure."

"I'll take some cookies if there are any going," Wiggles said.

Auntie Queenie bustled everyone into the large, well-used kitchen in my mom's house. We always ended up here whenever we had a family emergency. She set Uncle Kenny by the sink so he could clean himself up, then bustled around, fixing drinks and handing out cookies to everyone before sitting next to Uncle Kenny and taking hold of his hand.

He took a sip of whiskey and grimaced. He wasn't much of a drinker.

"You were hiding something from Dazielle when she interviewed you," I said.

He paused, his drink halfway to his mouth. "What makes you say that?"

"Because I know you, and you're a terrible liar. What did you see in the woods?"

Uncle Kenny set his drink down and placed his hands flat on the table. "I've already told you."

"Why were you even in the woods?" I said.

"You sound almost as bad as those angels. You must believe him," Auntie Queenie said.

"I believe he's innocent, but I don't believe you. You weren't with him tonight."

She waved a hand in the air. "I may as well have been. We know Kenny would never do anything like this. I'm happy to be his alibi. I trust him."

"So do I." I turned my attention back to Uncle Kenny. "But I still want to know what you hid from

Dazielle. You kept shuffling around in your seat. It made you look nervous."

"Of course, he's nervous. The angels have him pegged as a murder suspect," Auntie Queenie said. "You know what they're like when they settle on a suspect. They hound them until they give up. If it weren't for your work with the angels, there'd be dozens of innocent people behind bars for crimes they didn't commit."

"I know Uncle Kenny isn't a criminal, but I still want to know what he was doing in the woods," I said.

He sighed. "I didn't want to say anything, but I was out there for a reason."

"On your own?" I said.

Auntie Queenie opened her mouth to protest, but he patted the back of her hand.

"Yes, on my own. But I did hear noises and go take a look. I never expected to find a body."

"Okay. And you were telling the truth about seeing someone looking at the body?" I said.

He nodded. "I was."

"Do you know who that someone is?"

He looked at Auntie Queenie, and a bemused smile crossed his face. "I couldn't believe it. I never thought I'd see him around here, but he came."

Auntie Queenie leaned back in her chair. "Oh, my! You really got him to visit?"

I tapped my finger on top of the table. "Who is visiting? What's attacking these women? I've seen the bite marks on the victims. It wasn't a werewolf or a vampire. If it's a shifter, then I don't know what kind it is. The marks look human, although they'd

73

have to have a large mouth. The kind that could fit a whole cake."

"I can do that," Wiggles said. "Although I didn't bite those women."

"It's not a shifter," Uncle Kenny said. "Well, I suppose, technically, he is. He can change his form but not turn from man to beast. It's not a total transformation."

"It's a he?" I said. "Do you know this guy?"

"We've communicated a couple of times. He's not the easiest individual to talk to. He's reclusive."

"What are we talking about?" I said.

Uncle Kenny leaned forward. "A rare and unusual magic using creature. I've been keeping an eye on him for months. I tracked him once and got him to talk to me, only for a few minutes. I wanted him to know about Willow Tree Falls, so he knew there was a safe haven if he needed one."

"His timing is terrible," I said. "He arrives just when there's a pack of people hunting shifters in our woods."

"Yes, perhaps not his best move. I wonder what convinced him to come this way," Uncle Kenny said.

"How long has he been here?" I asked.

"Only a day or two. He keeps to himself. He doesn't want trouble, and I can't imagine him being involved in this murder."

"Uncle Kenny, what kind of creature are we talking about?"

He sucked in a breath, a smile of wonder on his face. "A Bigfoot."

I puffed out my surprise. "A Bigfoot, here?"

"I couldn't believe it when I first found clues he was in the area. I found evidence of his den and then fur and food remains."

"Bigfoot aren't meat eaters, are they?"

"No! They're herbivores. Roots, tubers, anything green, maybe the occasional bug. He's a gentle giant."

"Your uncle has always been interested in these creatures."

"So this Bigfoot moves into the village, and women are attacked," I said.

"It's a coincidence. They like the quiet life. It's why they're so rarely seen," Uncle Kenny said.

"Why didn't you tell Dazielle about the Bigfoot?" I said.

"Because she'd jump to the conclusion that he was the attacker."

"If he's anything like the pictures I've seen of Bigfoot, he fits the description the women gave of the creature that attacked them. They described him as a giant bear or a great ape with long fur."

"Oh! That does sound like Basil," Uncle Kenny said.

"It was Basil you saw standing over Sabine's body?" I said.

"It was. I called out to him, to let him know it was me, but he was startled. He ran away. For all I know, he could have seen the attack."

"You don't think he was involved, do you? Maybe Sabine scared him, and he bit her in self-defense."

"Bigfoot are less prone to violence than your Uncle Kenny," Auntie Queenie said.

I sank back into my seat. "Maybe, but something bad happened. Four women were bitten. One of them is dead, and now we have an unknown Bigfoot in the woods."

"Don't tell Dazielle about Basil," Uncle Kenny said. "I don't want her interrogating him. She'll frighten him, and he's not great at communicating. He could say the wrong thing and get in trouble."

"I'll keep quiet for now, but I need to talk to this Bigfoot."

"What we all need to do is rest," Auntie Queenie said. "Basil's not going anywhere. You can talk to him tomorrow. Besides, if you go poking around the woods again tonight, Dazielle will probably throw you both in a cell."

"He's safe for now," Uncle Kenny said. "I know where his den is. It's in the deepest part of the forest where no one will find him."

As much as I wanted to quiz Basil about what he saw and if he knew anything about biting random women, it was getting late, and I needed to check in at Cloven Hoof. "Okay, but I'll meet up with you tomorrow at noon. We need to talk to this Bigfoot and find out if he's got anything to do with these attacks."

Uncle Kenny nodded. "I promise you, he didn't kill Sabine."

I stood from my seat and headed to the door. "Maybe not, but he may know who did, and that makes him important and possibly the only way we can clear your name."

Uncle Kenny looked worried, while Auntie Queenie gave a satisfied nod.

"Tempest will sort this out," she said. "We have nothing to worry about."

I said my goodbyes and left with Wiggles. I wish I had half her confidence, but I'd do whatever I needed to do to keep Uncle Kenny safe.

Chapter 7

The next morning, I was making my way through a large stack of maple drizzled pancakes, while Wiggles finished his second bowl of dog food with pancakes on the side. So much for the chicken and rice diet.

I had a leather-bound book in front of me and was reading about Bigfoot. Or should that be Bigfeet? Was that the official plural for this elusive magic user?

"Bigfoot grow huge red manes when they're looking for a mate. The redder the mane, the hotter the Bigfoot. Well, the hotter the Bigfoot is to another Bigfoot," I said.

Wiggles mumbled something as he ate.

"Uh oh. This doesn't bode well for our furry friend." I tapped a picture in the book. "They have flat teeth. Their bite impressions would fit the ones on the victims."

Wiggles lifted his nose from his bowl. "I'm with your Uncle Kenny on this. Bigfoot are placid creatures. They don't need to attack people. If anyone sees them, they're terrified by their size.

And don't they have some weird ability to do with time?"

I kept reading. "You're right. It's called temporal stasis."

Wiggles trotted over and placed his front paws on my knee, taking a sniff at my pancakes. "That's it. They can stop time or something."

"Which gives them a chance to get away if anyone sees them," I said. "That's clever."

"And it's why so few people have ever encountered a Bigfoot or gotten a decent picture of one of them," Wiggles said. "If they get caught, they slow things down and make a run for it."

"That's a handy skill, but it also means our Bigfoot could easily sneak up on someone and attack them. Basil's got to be a suspect in this murder."

"But why bite those women? I thought Bigfoot weren't into juicy human steaks."

"Eww! That's gross. And they aren't." I shut the book and finished my pancakes, tossing Wiggles my last half. "We need to get out of here. Let's go grab Uncle Kenny and find Basil, see what he has to tell us."

We left the apartment and walked through the village. There were already small groups of people milling around, getting ready for a second day of hunting, so they could claim the reward money.

"Dazielle had better be on top of that lot," I said. "We don't want them tracking us while we find Basil."

"I wouldn't worry about them. It looks like most of them couldn't find their way out of a paper bag."

The crowds made me uneasy. There was a sense of vigilante justice in the air that meant things could quickly get out of hand.

We arrived at Mom's house to find Uncle Kenny already on the porch, pacing back and forth. It was one of the few times I'd seen him nervous. But he was a suspect in a murder investigation, so he had every right to feel unsettled.

He hurried down and joined us as we reached the gate. He was dressed in hiking clothes and had a backpack on. "Dazielle's been in touch. She wants to interview me again."

"I bet she does. Dazielle loves to focus on the easy clues and suspects she can easily break."

"You think I'd confess to something I didn't do?" He looked crestfallen.

I hugged him. "No! But she knows you're a gentle guy. She'll use that against you and try to make you say something that could incriminate you."

"I like peace, but I won't go to prison simply for a quiet life. I can handle Dazielle if I have to."

"I completely agree." My gaze ran over his clothing. "You're set up for a long hike. How far are we going?"

"It could take us a while to find Basil. He's based out past the swamp."

I grimaced as I looked at my favorite black boots. I should have worn something I wouldn't mind getting filthy.

We hurried away from the village and into the woods.

"I keep replaying what I saw last night," Uncle Kenny said. "Basil could have stumbled on the body, just like I did. Maybe he was trying to help Sabine."

"We'll have to ask him about that," I said. "And I was reading up on Bigfoot this morning to figure out why Basil may have wanted to harm her."

"They're amazing creatures. I've had an interest in them for a long time."

"Do they really have the ability to manipulate time?" I said.

"Oh, yes. It's called temporal stasis. I've even heard of a few powerful Bigfoot who can temporarily stop time. Most can simply slow it down, though."

"What do they use that ability for?"

"Nothing bad. At least, not from the reports I've read. Bigfoot don't enjoy company. They're on the extreme end of the introvert scale. They get exhausted if they're surrounded by company and only meet with other Bigfoot when it's mating time. The male locates the female, and once he's had his fun, he leaves her to rear the infant on her own."

"Hands-off parenting," I said. "I know a few guys who are like that."

Uncle Kenny chuckled. "It's the way they do things. Bigfoot don't thrive in the company of others. Combined with their desire to be alone and their ability to manipulate time, it makes them vulnerable. There are people out there who want to manipulate their ability. Imagine if you had a Bigfoot you could control. You'd be able to do pretty much whatever you liked."

"You could stop time and rob a bank," Wiggles said. "Although I'd rob my favorite cake store."

"If you had a creature with that power under your command, no one could hurt you. If anyone came at you, attacked you, or tried to shoot you, you'd get the Bigfoot to do his magic, and you could escape danger," Uncle Kenny said.

"I imagine Kirk Wrangler would be interested in those abilities. Do you think he knows Basil is here? Is that why he's causing such a stir?" I said.

"Kirk is the guy setting up the marquee?"

"And the hunting parties," I said. "I don't like him."

"It makes sense he'd be interested in finding a Bigfoot. But didn't he put up a reward to capture the creature dead or alive? A dead Bigfoot is no use to anyone."

I frowned. That was true, but it still didn't make me warm to Kirk.

After forty-five minutes of walking, we moved into the deepest part of the forest. The ground underfoot was increasingly squelchy, and it was getting difficult to yank my feet out of the oozing mud.

Wiggles started blasting out small fireballs to help dry the mud in front of him as he walked along. Uncle Kenny was fine with his walking boots and walking poles.

We continued along a barely visible path, having to push aside thick swathes of ivy that had wound around tree branches, slowly strangling them.

"We're getting close, so keep your voices down," Uncle Kenny said. "We don't want to startle him. He's had enough frights since finding Sabine. Bigfoot are emotionally intense creatures, and they feel the pain and distress of others deeply. It must have been terrible for him to discover Sabine's body."

It wouldn't have been so terrible if he'd been the one to kill her. Maybe he'd wanted her dead and was glad she was gone.

We crept forward, the trees overhead so dense it seemed more like dusk than early afternoon.

Wiggles paused and his ears flipped up. "There's something shuffling around in front of us."

"Let me go first," Uncle Kenny said. "He'll recognize me and won't be so afraid." He led the way along the now non-existent path.

We stopped at what appeared to be an impenetrable wall of greenery.

Uncle Kenny hunted around for a couple of minutes before pushing his hand through a tiny gap. We shuffled our way through more thick foliage.

My hair kept getting yanked on tree branches, and my feet were now sinking several inches into thick, gooey mud.

I popped out the other side into a part of the forest I'd never seen before. Huge weeping willows loomed around us, and in front of us was a dark opening that led into a cave.

"This is his home?" I whispered.

"It's the perfect refuge for a Bigfoot," Uncle Kenny whispered back. "Quiet, isolated, and hard to get to."

I took a step forward, but my foot remained glued in the mud. I tried to pull it free, but it wasn't just my foot stuck. My body didn't want to work. I inched my way down my leg with my fingers, fighting each movement as my limbs felt frozen and heavy.

"It's Basil." Uncle Kenny's words emerged slowly from his mouth. "He's using his ability. He must have heard us coming."

"Tell him to stop." I sank another inch into the mud. This would end badly if I couldn't break free of Basil's magic. I'm talking being slowly swallowed by a swamp and meeting a sticky, muddy demise kind of ending.

"Basil, it's Kenny. We don't mean you harm." It took about a minute for him to say that sentence, and the whole time, I continued to sink.

Smoke slowly plumed out of Wiggles' mouth, but he also wasn't moving.

I could do nothing but stare as a huge dark shadow loomed out of the cave. The ground underfoot shook as Basil approached.

Slowly, I tilted my head up. Basil was huge. At least seven foot tall, with massive shoulders and dazzling green eyes. And although he had long dark hair that looked dreadlocked and was tied off of his face, he didn't have the appearance of a shaggy ape at all. He looked like a rather gorgeous warrior type. All he was missing was the loin cloth. He had on pants, just like a normal guy, but his chest was bare, despite how chilly it was.

Basil's gaze flicked around us. "Kenny, why have you brought these creatures here?" His voice was a deep, low rumble in his broad chest.

"They're part of my family," Kenny said. "We're here to help."

Basil lifted a large hand and swiped it down his face. He studied me first then Wiggles. He lifted his hand again and rotated it in a circle twice.

My ears popped and I could move again. I yanked my feet out of the mud and shook out the pins and needles that had begun in my toes.

"Thanks, Basil," Kenny said. "We didn't mean to intrude, but I thought you could use some assistance. This is my niece, Tempest Crypt, and that's Wiggles."

Basil nodded at us both, his expression one of suspicion. "You shouldn't have come here."

"You're in danger," I said. "People are looking for you."

He shook his head. "People are always looking for me. They're so fascinated by Bigfoot. I wish they'd leave us alone. That's all we want, to be left in peace, to live our lives without being the object of scrutiny. It's uncomfortable living under a spotlight you have no interest in."

"I'm sorry to say, you won't get peace here, not now a woman's been murdered," I said.

Basil's face flushed a deep red. "I didn't do it. I found her, but that's all."

"What were you doing in the woods last night?" I said. "You must have known about Kirk and his hunting parties. They weren't being discreet."

Basil stroked a hand over a long red streak that ran through his hair. "I wasn't worried about them. I shouldn't be forced into hiding because there are ill-informed idiots chasing after me. And I kept to myself. I just needed to get out. I should be allowed to go wherever I like." He shuddered and a thin layer of hair covered him for a few seconds, before disappearing.

I blinked. "I was wondering where your fur was. You can make yourself look almost human whenever you like?"

"I can. It helps me blend in. I sort of fit into the shifter category, but they're not keen on me hanging around them because of the whole time slowing thing. It makes them nervous. There's nothing I can do about my height, though," he said. "Not that I want to blend in all that often, but when I leave my dwelling, I try not to draw attention."

"Basil, I saw you standing over Sabine's body," Uncle Kenny said. "Did you see anything? Was there someone attacking her when you arrived?"

"No! I found her on the ground. I thought I might be able to help, but she'd lost a lot of blood. I don't know how to revive a human. I pressed on her chest a few times and watched to see if she started to breathe, but she didn't."

"Someone bit her," I said. "Are you sure you don't know anything about that?"

His face flushed again. "No. I heard someone coming and ran off before I was seen."

"That was me," Uncle Kenny said. "You didn't hear me call out your name?"

"I was too panicked to think straight. I feel bad. Maybe I could have done more to help that woman."

"I don't think you could," Uncle Kenny said. "She was dead when I got there. And as you noted, she'd already lost a lot of blood."

"Whoever bit her must have hit an artery," I said. "The other bite victims didn't lose that much blood.

This attack seems different. Something must have gone wrong."

"Maybe Sabine fought back," Uncle Kenny said.

I nodded. "It looked like she'd struggled. Her clothes were dirty, and there was blood smeared on her. Maybe our biter only meant to injure her, but when she didn't turn out to be a meek little thing, he got nasty and savaged her."

"I don't know anything about that," Basil said. "And I don't know how I can help. I just want to leave this place. I should never have visited, but Kenny made it sound so peaceful."

"You shouldn't go anywhere for now," Uncle Kenny said. "There are groups everywhere, all fired up to catch the killer."

"And if they see you sprouting fur and lumbering toward them, they'll go crazy," I said.

Basil lifted his chin. "I don't lumber. I may be large, but I'm not clumsy."

"Bigfoot are elegant for their size," Uncle Kenny murmured.

"Okay, Mr. Light on his Toes, but you still haven't answered the question about what you were doing in the woods. I get the freedom to roam argument, but it wasn't the smartest move," I said.

Basil huffed out a breath. "I was taking a walk."

"You weren't bothered about all those troublemakers roaming about and wanting to bag themselves a creature?" There was brave and carefree, and then there was plain foolish. I didn't have Basil down as the dumb, furry, beastie type.

"I had energy to burn off." He stroked the red stripe running through his hair again. "I wasn't looking for trouble, and I kept away from the groups. If any of them came near me, I slowed things down so I could make my escape."

"You were alone that whole time?" I said.

"I was," Basil said. "There's no one around here I like to spend time with. Although I don't object to Kenny."

"I appreciate you taking your time with me," Uncle Kenny said.

"You're one of the few people I can tolerate being around," Basil said. "I'm already getting a headache from interacting with you."

"Why don't you like talking to us?" I said. "Have you got something to hide?"

"I don't enjoy talking at all. It's not how Bigfoot normally communicate."

"How do you communicate?" I must have missed that when I was cramming for my Bigfoot 101 exam.

Basil looked at Wiggles. "May I use you for an experiment? It won't hurt. Although you may feel a slight tickle."

"Err, I guess so." Wiggles walked over to Basil. "What are you going to do?"

Basil touched the tip of his finger to Wiggles' forehead. "This is how we prefer to communicate."

There was a long silence as Basil crouched in front of Wiggles, keeping his finger pressed against his head.

"What are they doing?" I whispered to Uncle Kenny.

He gave a soft laugh. "Extraordinary. I've read about this method of communication, but I've never seen it done. It's zoolingualism. It's the power to communicate with other animals."

"Basil's talking to Wiggles without using words?" That was a neat skill.

"Yes. Wiggles is hearing the words in his head. It's remarkable."

"What's he saying to you?" I said to Wiggles.

Wiggles kept his head still but shifted his eyes. "The guy's really sad. All he wants is to be accepted. Can we adopt him? We can make room for him in the apartment. I can get him a bed next to mine."

I shook my head. There was no way Basil was moving in.

Uncle Kenny sighed. "If it makes you feel better, Basil, you're not the only suspect in this investigation. The angels are also interested in me."

"Which is the dumbest idea they've ever had," I said. "You were trying to help Sabine."

"So was I." Basil removed his finger from Wiggles' head.

"The problem is, they only have our words for that," Uncle Kenny said.

"You have Auntie Queenie as your dodgy alibi," I said. "And I trust you. You'd never do anything like that. But I don't know Basil."

"I'll vouch for him," Uncle Kenny said. "And Queenie shouldn't have given me an alibi. We've spoken about that. She panicked and wanted to make sure I wouldn't get in trouble. Although if we're not careful, she'll be the one in trouble with the angels. Dazielle is a stickler for the rules."

"Which is why I'm working with them to make sure we bend those rules enough so people like you don't get accused of murder."

Basil's shoulders slumped, and he lowered his head. "I thought I'd be safe here. Other magic users always say it's the perfect place and welcomes everyone."

"We do. Unfortunately, we can't stop the tourists from coming, and they're not always so welcoming," I said.

"Most of them are fine," Uncle Kenny said. "But for now, Basil, you need to stay hidden."

"Which means no more midnight strolls," I said.

Basil adjusted his dreadlocks. "Very well. And if it's any help, I saw Sabine before she died."

"You were watching her?" I said.

"No! Well, she was a pretty woman. I notice beauties like Sabine. I was worried about her because she was arguing with the guy in charge of the magic exhibition. I don't like him."

"Kirk Wrangler," I said. "He has that effect on everyone he meets."

"Yes, that's the name I heard. They were looking for a spot to place the large marquee and came close to the woods. I happened to be passing by—"

"Lurking to get a peek of Sabine?"

Basil had the good grace to blush. "Perhaps I was admiring her. I'd have left them alone, but the conversation grew intense. Kirk started yelling, and I wanted to make sure Sabine was okay."

"What were they arguing about?"

"He was threatening her. Warning her to keep quiet about something, or she'd lose her job."

"Did Sabine have dirt on Kirk? Was she threatening to reveal it and he didn't like that?" I looked at Uncle Kenny, and he shrugged.

"Kirk didn't say what Sabine should keep quiet about, but she wasn't happy. She kept saying it wasn't right, and they had to stop. Her sadness wounded me. Humans feel their emotions so intensely that I stay away from them, but I was drawn to this one. Her loneliness made me feel like we could be kindred spirits."

"How drawn to her were you?" I said. "Enough to make a move?"

Basil looked away. "I can appreciate human beauty."

"You're into humans?"

He muttered something under his breath.

Uncle Kenny cleared his throat. "It's not outside the realm of possibility."

Humans and Bigfoot! I guess I'd heard of odder matches. But Basil concerned me. He didn't have a good alibi, and he'd admitted to liking the look of Sabine.

"Do me a favor and show me your teeth," I said to Basil.

He took a step back. "Why do you need to see my teeth?"

"Because Sabine was bitten."

He waved his hands in the air and shook his head. "She had those marks on her when I found her."

"And Bigfoot don't attack people," Uncle Kenny said. "They're peaceful."

"We are. I never cause anyone pain."

Despite Basil's reluctance to show me his teeth, I could see enough of them to know they were flat. He wasn't off the hook just yet.

"My head is pounding," Basil said. "I need to rest."

"That's enough questioning for now," Uncle Kenny said to me. "Bigfoot are sensitive. We don't want to scare Basil, so he runs off."

Basil was shaking all over as more fur sprouted out of him.

I felt sorry for the guy. He did seem to be a gentle giant. I could always come back if I needed more information. "Don't go anywhere, Basil. I may have more questions for you."

Basil shuddered and nodded his head. "I won't leave."

"It's not safe for you to be moving around, anyway," Uncle Kenny said, "not until the crowds leave. We'll come back and let you know when it's quieter."

He sighed, turned, and headed back inside the cave.

"What do you make of Basil?" Uncle Kenny led the way back through the trees.

"He seems more confused than anything. But I'm not happy he was watching Sabine. It's a bit creepy. And his alibi is terrible."

"Bigfoot and humans aren't dissimilar," Uncle Kenny said. "Apart from the size difference and excess hair, they could be compatible in a romantic encounter."

"You think Basil had a crush on Sabine?"

"Why not? Basil likes to be alone most of the time, but every lonely bachelor needs a little love."

I grinned. Uncle Kenny was such a romantic.

"Let's leave Basil alone for now. I've got another target to focus on, one I'd much rather discover is guilty. It's time to talk to Kirk Wrangler again. If he's involved in this, I'll make him sorry for messing with you, Basil, and Willow Tree Falls."

Chapter 8

I walked back to the house with Uncle Kenny and Wiggles. We said goodbye, and I headed to the marquee with Wiggles to find Kirk and grill him.

As I walked up the hill, there was a large crowd gathered outside the marquee. I settled in near the back and waited to see what was happening.

"It could be one of three beasts. They're all dangerous and need to be handled with extreme care." Kirk stood at the front of the crowd. He was dressed like he was about to join the army, in combat fatigues and a fitted dark green T-shirt that didn't hide his slight dad paunch. Beside him were large illustrations of different shifters. There was a werewolf, an enormous black bear, and a huge panther.

Excitement radiated off the crowd as they listened to Kirk.

"How do we kill these creatures?" one guy asked.

"They require different methods of elimination," Kirk said. "The bear shifter can only be killed by having its head chopped off. The wolf needs a silver bullet through the heart."

"That's just a giant wolf, though, isn't it?" a woman asked. "They aren't really... shifters. They can't turn back into people, can they?" She glanced around her.

"Don't be so quick to discount werewolves or any kind of shape shifting beast," Kirk said. "After all, aren't you all here to learn about the world of magic?"

There was a general mutter of agreement from the crowd.

Kirk gestured to the marquee behind him. "Those of you who have yet to visit my exhibition will have your eyes opened once you come inside. Perhaps then you'll be ready to believe in the supernatural. Our beast could simply be a wild wolf, grown to an enormous size and vicious beyond all recognition. But what if it is something more? You need to be prepared for that if you're joining a hunting party."

"And we only get this bounty if we catch the thing?" someone else called out from the front of the crowd.

"That's right. And I'd prefer the creature alive. It would make for a fascinating addition to my work. But such a beast is hard to control, even in my experienced hands."

"This guy's ego is bigger than that marquee," Wiggles muttered.

I scowled at Kirk as he continued to stir up the crowd and spout nonsense. "We need to shut him down before he incites a riot and we have idiots with weapons racing around the woods shooting each other." I eased through the crowd until I was at the front.

Kirk was still waxing lyrical about shifter bears and how they were more dangerous than normal bears. He had no clue what he was talking about. They were only dangerous when they got hungry or if you tried to steal their food. Shifter bears were gentle creatures.

"Do all these beasts have fangs?" I said.

Kirk glanced at me. He looked at his shoes and shuffled back a step. "They do. It makes them lethal."

"I heard the victim was bitten, but there were no fang marks on her body. How do you explain that?" I felt dozens of pairs of eyes settle on me.

Kirk raised his eyebrows. "How do you know about the bite marks?"

"I work with the police in the village."

"Ah! Well, my understanding is that my assistant, Sabine, is still being examined by the appropriate authorities. Unless you examined her."

"I didn't, but I have access to the police records. Sabine wasn't killed by any of these creatures. The bite marks on her body are wrong. You're not looking for a wild animal, or did you say a shifter? Isn't that something out of a comic?"

Kirk hesitated and looked around the crowd. Seeming satisfied by what he saw, he smirked at me. "Sabine deserves justice. You and the police are acting too slowly. If this creature isn't caught, there'll be another death. I have all these willing people here to help solve your problem. We want to help. We want to make your village a safe place. You would deny us that?"

"You can help by leaving," I said.

A grumble ran through the crowd. It sounded angry and aimed at me.

Kirk clapped his hands together. "That's enough for today, everyone. These creatures are most active at night, so that's when we'll send out the first hunting parties. I have lists with your names on them inside the tent to your left. Go check which party you're with then let me know if you need weapons."

The crowd slowly broke up, and Kirk spent a couple of minutes talking to people before striding over to me.

"I want a word with you," he said.

"Good, because I want to talk to you, too."

"Why did you break those artifacts?"

I tilted my head. "What are you talking about?"

"You came here yesterday poking around, and after you left, I found one of the display tents full of broken artifacts. Did you do that?"

I'd almost forgotten Zandra had smashed a display. "That had nothing to do with me."

"I'm not so sure. And one of the workers hasn't shown up today. Did you convince her to leave?"

I suppose I had, but I wasn't going to tell Kirk I was related to Zandra. "You've lost me. And I'm not here to talk about your artifacts or your missing teammates. You need to stop stirring up trouble. These people don't know what they're dealing with. Sending groups out to hunt a wild animal, or a werewolf, or whatever you think it is, could mean they get hurt. Just like Sabine."

A dark flush spread up Kirk's cheeks. "She's the reason I'm doing this."

"Is that the truth? Or are you looking to have some poor wild animal's head mounted on your wall?"

Kirk shrugged. "It's only right the beast is displayed for everyone to see." He looked down at Wiggles and scowled. "I hope that thing isn't going to be sick again. You owe me a new pair of shoes."

"I'll see what I can find in the thrift store," I said. "You don't seem distressed about Sabine's death. Didn't you like her?"

He glanced around before stepping closer. "It's always disappointing to lose a reliable assistant."

"You weren't friends?"

"She was an employee, nothing more. She hadn't been with me that long. Maybe six months."

"From what I've heard, you didn't treat her well," I said.

"I treated her fine. If she did the work I needed, she was rewarded. That's how this employment business works."

"I have a witness who saw you arguing with Sabine not long before she was killed."

Kirk snorted a laugh. "What witness? Whoever it is, they're lying."

"I believe the witness, and he has no reason to lie. You were heard warning Sabine to keep quiet about something. What would that be?"

He was quiet for a few seconds. "Sometimes, Sabine needed reminding of her job, that's all. Now, she's gone, I'll have to start over again. It's a nuisance having to find another assistant and break her in."

I recoiled. Kirk really was a jerk. Kirk the jerk. That had a satisfying ring to it.

"Did Sabine have something on you that you didn't want getting out?"

"No! If your witness told you that, he's an idiot, and you shouldn't believe him. He's jealous of my success. He wants to ruin me by spreading lies."

"He isn't jealous of you. Where were you when Sabine was killed?" I said.

Kirk rubbed his hands together. "That's an easy one."

"Out in the woods on a hunting expedition?"

"I'm sorry to disappoint you, but I tend to stay out of the hunts. I've enjoyed my fair share in the past but decided to let other people have fun."

"So, where were you?"

"At a restaurant that was open late. The woman running the place was doing a deal for visitors and holding late-night sittings so they could come in after they'd been in the forest. I enjoyed a pleasant hour there chatting to the owner. She was delightful."

There was only one restaurant that stayed open late. It was Tilly's. "You mean Tilly's restaurant, Bite Me?"

"Yes. And I plan to go back. Tilly was very welcoming, if you know what I mean." Kirk's tongue slid across his bottom lip.

I didn't believe his alibi for a second. And there'd be no way Tilly would waste her time on a loser like this.

My gaze ran over Kirk. He oozed arrogance. I really wanted him to be the killer. "If you weren't involved with what happened to Sabine—"

"Which I wasn't."

"Who do you think killed her?"

He shrugged. "It was the wild beast roaming around the village. I'm surprised it hasn't attacked before. Or maybe it has, and it's been covered up so it doesn't put off tourists. People do shady things for money."

He should know. "The creatures in our woods don't attack us because we leave them alone. It's only when we get groups of ill-informed tourists blundering around that there are problems. A problem you're not helping."

"So you admit you do have rare creatures in your forest." Kirk's smile was smug. "What have you seen? Are there really werewolves here?"

I shook my head. "There are plenty of wild animals. They hate it when people stamp around and disturb their homes. And they'd probably like to take a bite out of anyone who gets in their way."

"If it's not a werewolf, what about a large cat? I've read plenty about abnormal creatures that can shift form."

"It's not a cat, or a wolf, or a bear. You need to stop your hunting parties, or someone else will get hurt."

"This is too important for my work. You may freelance for the police, but you don't tell me what to do," Kirk said. "There's a monster out there, and I will catch it."

"What if you're the monster we're looking for?"

He scowled at me. "Hassle someone else. How about the thing Sabine told me was stalking her?"

"A thing?"

"Yes! She said she saw something in the woods peering at her."

"What did it look like?"

Kirk crossed his arms over his chest. "Oh, so you believe me now?"

"No, I'm humoring you. What did it look like?"

"Some kind of giant dog. It scared Sabine. And she'd support this hunt. She'd want the beast destroyed. Now, I need to go. I have hunting parties to coordinate." He turned and marched away.

"He's a big lying jerk," Wiggles said.

"Kirk's lying about a lot of things. There's no way Tilly would look twice at him. And he denied arguing with Sabine until I mentioned Basil had seen them fighting."

"We need to talk to Tilly and blow his alibi apart," Wiggles said. "And if we time it right, she should have food going spare."

I checked the time. "We'll have to do it tomorrow. I need to get to Cloven Hoof. It's Zandra's first night, and I need to show her the ropes. But Kirk is definitely on the top of my suspect list." I turned and headed back down the hill toward Cloven Hoof.

"The way he talks, it sounds like he believes in shifters," Wiggles said. "Do you think he's ever seen one?"

"He knows something, but he has no respect for magic, he just wants to exploit it. That's not the behavior of a true magic user."

I dashed through the doors of the club ten minutes later and looked around.

Merrie Noble and two other bar staff were already in, getting things ready for opening.

"Hey, has someone called Zandra shown up? She's a new hire." I dropped onto a stool by the bar.

"No one's come in yet," Merrie said. "What's going on by the stone circle?"

I groaned. "Bad news. Someone wants to go out hunting our shifters."

Her eyes widened a fraction. "Are they crazy?"

"Most likely. Hit me with a lemon drop, and I'll tell you all about it."

Twenty minutes later, and after two lemon drops, Merrie knew all about Sabine, Kirk, and the hunting parties. And Zandra still hadn't shown up.

"I'll be in the office," I said to Merrie as I headed away from the bar. "If Zandra arrives, point her in my direction."

"Sure thing, boss."

I spent an hour tackling paperwork, getting increasingly annoyed that Zandra hadn't appeared. I was giving her a chance by offering her this job, and she'd already let me down.

Wiggles lifted his head from his paws. "Someone's coming."

There was a tap on the door, and it was pushed open. Zandra stood outside.

"Where have you been?" I said. "I wanted to show you how everything worked before people came in tonight."

"I lost track of time." She ambled in and looked around. "This is where you hide out when you're not pounding demons into the ground?"

I pushed back my seat and stood. "I don't have time to show you everything now. You can start on clean-up duties tonight."

"Clean-up? Like the washrooms?"

I was tempted to make her do that job, since she'd been so late. "You can start by going around the tables, making sure everything is tidy and collecting empty glasses. This way." We headed back out into the club.

There were a couple of regulars already in, but it was quiet this early in the evening. I gave Zandra a quick tour, then showed her the washer where the empty glasses were stacked and cleaned.

She walked around, not saying much, but I could sense she wasn't happy.

"Any questions?" I stopped by the bar.

"I will get to do other things, though? I don't just want to collect empty glasses."

"If we don't have clean glasses, people can't get anything to drink. Besides, we all have to start somewhere. It's a job. Better than working for a sleazy murder suspect."

Her eyebrows shot up. "You think Kirk's a killer?"

"He's on my suspect list. Right at the top."

Her gaze ran over me. "I noticed you spend a lot of time with the angels."

"I sort of work with them," I said. "Which is why I often need extra hands here."

"How do you know it was Kirk who killed Sabine?"

"I don't know for sure, but he's hiding things, and I don't like his alibi."

"I didn't like the guy either. Have you spoken to Sabine's bestie about him? Bella something or other."

"No, not yet. Why do you think I should talk to her?"

"After the accident with the artifacts, I realized I'd left my coat behind. I slipped back to the marquee to get it and saw Sabine hanging out with her friends. She seemed tight with them. Bella and some blond guy whose name I didn't catch. Maybe Sabine told Bella something to help you figure out what happened."

I patted Zandra's shoulder. "Thanks. That's useful. I'll check her out."

"Maybe I can help with the murder investigation. It would be more interesting than collecting dirty glasses."

I shook my head. There was no way I was dragging Zandra into the middle of this mystery. "You get started here. Come on. It's time to get to work."

Chapter 9

It was late the next morning, and I hadn't long come down from the apartment over the club. I did a slow circuit of the main room, a frown on my face.

Merrie hurried through the main door.

I blinked at her in surprise. "You're not supposed to be here for hours."

She set down her purse and tugged off her jacket. "Well, after how awful last night was, I figured you could do with some help."

I scrubbed my fingers through my hair. "It really was terrible, wasn't it?"

Merrie walked over with a broom in her hand and patted my arm. "Zandra was trying. She just took offence quickly when the customers joked with her. I'm sure she'll get the hang of things." She set to work cleaning up broken glass from under a table. It was one of many glasses Zandra had dropped. She'd destroyed so many, I had to wonder if she'd done it deliberately, so I'd give her something else to do.

And she hadn't just been clumsy. She'd used her magic inappropriately and had been rude to customers.

"Maybe she's not meant for the club business," I said.

Merrie glanced up at me. "You have to have a thick skin when working in a place like this. When people drink too much, their inhibitions fall. They say dumb things and occasionally make an inappropriate grab or two. You get used to it."

"Do people inappropriately grab you?" I wouldn't stand for my team being messed around by idiots.

"They only ever do it once." Merrie grinned at me. "That is unless they want their shoulder dislocated and a lifetime ban."

I smiled back at her. Merrie always knew how to handle the clientele. "How was Zandra with you?"

She bit her bottom lip. "She doesn't like being told how to do things. I get it, she's young and thinks she knows it all. But she kept stacking the glass washer wrong. I had to keep redoing it when her back was turned so they wouldn't break. It meant customers waited at the bar longer than they needed to. She even tried to serve some drinks. One of her concoctions exploded in front of a customer, and he almost lost his eyebrows. I gave him a free round to keep him happy."

I dropped my head in my hands and rubbed my forehead. "I told Zandra to stay out from behind the bar. It's way too soon for that. We're mixing magic into the drinks. You need a careful touch."

Merrie leaned on the broom. "I got the impression Zandra isn't experienced with controlling her magic. She has a lot of it, it was practically oozing from her pores, especially when she got angry. She's got power, but it's not safe to use around our customers."

"I'll make sure she doesn't do it again," I said. "Thanks for helping out with her last night."

"You're going to keep her on? Maybe we could find someone else more suited for this kind of work. I can ask around."

I was sure there was, but I wanted to give Zandra a second chance. It was never easy starting a new job, but she needed to stop using her magic. I didn't want her scaring away my customers or injuring them.

"I'll get her back in on a quiet night, when she can break as much as she likes, and we don't need to worry about the customers getting harmed."

Merrie shrugged and kept sweeping the broken glass. "Whatever you say."

Feeling more than a little guilty for giving Merrie extra work, I spent the next couple of hours helping. By the time I left the club with Wiggles, you'd hardly know my half-sister had rampaged through the place with her magic and sharp comments.

"I hope we're going for a huge second breakfast after all that work," Wiggles said.

"I don't know why you're hungry. You fell asleep in a booth while we were cleaning. You didn't lift a paw to help."

"It was exhausting watching you work. Now, I'm starving."

I could do with some fuel after the cleaning marathon. "Let's combine food and suspect hunting."

"I like that plan," Wiggles said. "Who are we interrogating, and where are we going to eat?"

"Zandra gave me an idea last night. It would be good to speak to Sabine's friends. She could have confided in them about something worrying her. Let's start with Bella. She seemed friendly when we met. And I expect she could do with comforting since she's lost her best buddy."

I discovered Bella leaving the hotel in the village, a glum expression on her face.

"Hey, it's Bella, isn't it?" I hurried over to her.

She glanced up, her eyes red-rimmed and her mouth downcast. "That's right. Do I know you?"

"No, but we met briefly when I was talking to Sabine in the marquee."

"Oh! You knew Sabine?"

"Not really. I'm sorry about what happened to her."

Bella sighed. "Me too. We were best friends. I can't believe this is real." She dabbed at her eyes with a tissue.

"I'm working with the local police on the investigation. Have you got time for a chat?"

"Oh! Of course." Bella's forehead crinkled. "But what's to investigate? She was attacked by a wild animal."

"We're looking into all possibilities. How about we go for a coffee and cake? You must need cheering up."

She sniffed and blotted at her nose with the tissue. "I don't think any amount of cake will cheer me up, but I wouldn't mind a strong coffee. I barely slept last night. I was going back home, but Oakley decided to stay, and I didn't want to leave him on his own. He's not taken the news well. Neither of us have."

"I don't blame you. If something bad happened to my best friend, I'd be demanding answers. Come with me. I've got the perfect quiet place where we can talk." I led Bella to Tilly's restaurant. Her cake was always delicious, and once I was done talking to Bella, I could check Kirk's alibi.

Wiggles was forced to wait outside, much to his disgust. Tilly wasn't a fan of fur in the food, but I quietly promised him a treat if he behaved.

We settled in a seat by the window and took a few minutes to look over the menu.

"Tempest. How's everything going?" Tilly walked over, a smile on her face.

"Everything's good with me. This is Bella. It was her friend who was attacked in the woods," I said.

"I heard about that. I'm so sorry." Tilly placed a hand on Bella's shoulder.

"I figured some of your amazing cake may help a little," I said. "What can you recommend?"

"I've got a red velvet cake with chocolate sauce. I just finished making it," Tilly said.

"What do you reckon, Bella?" I said.

"That does sound good. And your strongest coffee, please."

"Make that two," I said.

"Coming right up." Tilly winked at me and walked away. She could probably guess I was here on official snooping business and would want to hear everything the second she could.

"Why don't you tell me a bit about Sabine?" I said to Bella. "How long had you known each other?"

"We'd been best friends since school."

"How did you meet?"

"I was being bullied by this mean girl, when Sabine marched in, completely fearless, and knocked her over. She grabbed my hand, and we ran off. She's been my heroine ever since. We did everything together after that. We even went to the same university and got a place together." She chuckled. "And this is silly, but we even shared the same imaginary friends."

"Imaginary friends?"

Bella gave me a sheepish smile. "You know, lots of kids have made up friends they talk to. One day, Sabine introduced me to the pixies living at the bottom of her garden. She said they'd always lived there and we should be friends with them. Sabine would take them food and gifts of colored stones. I was happy to play along."

Tilly returned with our coffee and cake, giving me a minute to mull over Bella's comments. Maybe Sabine had magic and had seen those pixies for real. They loved colored glass and stones.

"Did Sabine have any problems at work?" I asked.

Bella shook her head. "Well, Kirk was an idiot. Sabine said he loved to yell at people, so she kept out of his way."

"Was she scared of him?"

"No, but he had an ego. She avoided him when she could. It worked most of the time. And she loved that job, even though the pay wasn't great."

I sampled the cake and almost groaned with pleasure at the rich, velvety chocolate explosion firing in my mouth. Tilly was a genius with her cakes.

Bella smiled. "It's great cake. Thanks for bringing me here."

I returned her smile. "When I saw Sabine with Oakley, they seemed close. Were they more than friends?"

Bella nodded as she ate another bite of cake. "Oakley and Bella dated for years. I figured they'd eventually get married."

"It went wrong?"

"Sabine was worried she was too young to settle down. She met Oakley at university, and he was her first serious boyfriend. He's a great guy but could be too relaxed at times. He loves to kick back and navel gaze. Sabine was worried he didn't have any ambition and she'd end up supporting him. They both have history degrees, and there's not much work that pays well with that qualification."

"Sabine didn't want a layabout as a husband?"

"Pretty much. They even argued about it a few times. Oakley promised he'd change, but Sabine didn't want to spend the rest of her life struggling to make ends meet while Oakley messed around with projects he'd never finish."

"She left him?"

"She did. They were sad about it for a while, and it was difficult to begin with because we were all friends. I felt like piggy in the middle, trying to divide my time between them."

"You didn't mind Oakley was taking your best friend away from you?"

Bella's eyebrows lifted. "Of course not. I like him, and I loved Sabine. I only wanted to see her happy. Most of the time, Oakley did just that. They were good together, but I supported her when she decided they needed to split up. Oakley took the break-up hard. It took him a few months to get his head together."

"He still seemed keen on Sabine when I saw them together," I said.

Bella took a sip of her coffee. "It was my suggestion we visit Sabine while she was working at the marquee. We only live fifty miles away, so it was an easy drive. I figured it was time they were friends again. I don't know. Maybe he did want her back, but he never said anything to me. I hope I didn't make things awkward between them."

"Do you think Oakley was holding a grudge because Sabine left him?" I said.

Her nose wrinkled. "Oakley doesn't hold grudges. He's chilled out about everything."

"You don't think he was angry about being dumped? Angry enough to do something about it?"

Bella lowered her coffee mug and shook her head. "Absolutely not. He's gutted about what happened to Sabine. He'd never want to see her hurt. Even though they weren't together, he cared about what she did. No, it's impossible he was involved. And we were together that evening. We'd gone for a walk around the village while Sabine was working and planned to meet up with her later. She never showed, which was weird because she was always so reliable."

"What time were you meeting with Sabine?" I said.

"Kirk had her working late, and she was due to finish at eleven-thirty that night. I'd been wandering around with Oakley. We grabbed a late dinner and had a couple of drinks at the pub. We headed to the marquee to see if Sabine was finished but couldn't find her. My phone's not been working since I got here, so I couldn't call to see where she was. We figured Kirk was keeping her late."

"What did you do then?"

"We headed back to the hotel. We met a group of people who told us about an attack in the woods and to stay inside. I didn't panic at first. Sabine was always the sensible one and would never go wandering in the woods late at night."

"But that's where she was found," I said. "And I was one of the first to find her."

Bella's eyes widened and then filled with tears. "I didn't know that. How was she? I mean, that's a silly question. Do you think she suffered? The police aren't telling me much."

I suppressed a grimace. I was never great at giving out bad news. "I'm not going to lie. She was probably scared. I think Sabine fought back."

Bella was quiet as she swirled her coffee in the mug. "It's so unfair. She was a sweet person. I don't know what I'll do without her in my life. I always imagined us being two awesome ladies growing old together. We'd have had so much fun. We could have drunk too much wine, eaten cake, and given a home to loads of cats. Now, she's gone, it'll never happen." Tears trickled down her face.

"We'll figure out what happened to Sabine," I said.

"You have to find that wild animal," Bella said. "It can't attack anyone else."

"There are people looking for it. If there's a dangerous animal out there, we'll catch it." Of course, Sabine's murder may be more complicated than that, possibly involving an ex-boyfriend who wanted her back, but she'd refused his advances. I needed to talk to Oakley. "Have you spoken to any of Sabine's family?"

"No. Sabine was adopted when she was small. She doesn't have any family left. We were sort of each other's family, just the three of us."

"Are you sticking around for a while?"

"Yes. Oakley and I have rooms at the hotel, and we can stay as long as we need to. I don't want to go anywhere until this is solved. I need to see the evil creature's head on a pole. That's what it deserves." Bella pushed her plate away and sighed. "Thanks for this. It's good to talk about what happened. I always talked through my problems with Sabine. I have Oakley, but it's not the same thing. Actually, I should see how he's doing. He didn't answer his door when I knocked this morning."

"I'm happy I could help you. And if you have trouble getting information out of the police, just come to me. I work with them on a freelance basis, so I can tell you more."

"Great. I'll do that. Thanks, Tempest." She pulled out her purse.

"No, this is on me. And try not to worry too much. We'll get to the bottom of this."

Bella nodded a goodbye, stood up, and headed out the door.

The second she'd gone, Tilly rushed over. "Tell me everything." She sat in the empty seat, an expectant look on her face.

I smiled at her. "What have you already heard?"

"That someone was savaged in the woods by a giant bear. It wasn't a shifter attack, was it?"

"I can confirm it wasn't a shifter. The bite marks look human."

"A human is biting people?" Tilly grimaced. "Have we got a cannibal on our hands?"

"No, but we have got a serial biter. Before Sabine was killed, more women were bitten. They had the same bite marks on their necks and in the same place."

"Which is weird," Tilly said. "What do you think is going on?"

"You may be able to help me with that puzzle. On the night of Sabine's murder, one of the suspects claims he was here, flirting with you."

"You know I never flirt with my customers. Well, only the super good-looking ones, and only if they leave a big tip." Tilly's eyes twinkled. "Describe him to me. It was busy that night, so I had a lot of people come through the restaurant."

"His name's Kirk Wrangler. He's the genius who brought the marquee into the village and is stirring up the hunters. He's tall, mid-forties, has slicked back dark hair and usually wears a suit. And he likes expensive shoes."

"I know who you're talking about. He was here late that night. He got in at the last sitting. He was smarmy and kept trying to flirt with me, but I brushed it off. He was way too smug and not my type. You know I like my guys more rugged."

I sighed. "That's not good news."

"That I like rugged guys or that Kirk was here?"

"The Kirk factor. I wanted him to have killed Sabine. I don't like the guy, and I hate the fact he's brought trouble to the village. Maybe Sabine would still be alive if he hadn't gotten groups rampaging through the woods."

"I see what you mean, but I'm sorry to say, it couldn't have been him. He was one of the last to leave that night. I had to encourage him out the door. Kirk didn't leave here till gone midnight."

"Then it wasn't him. It's a pity, I could have had him arrested and then shut down his exhibition and gotten rid of the visitors."

"You know the real pity?"

"What's that?"

"That Rhett's not around to help with this investigation. He knows the woods well." Tilly arched an eyebrow. "Any news about him?"

"I'm not thinking about Rhett. He left the village without even telling me."

"Ouch! That's not good. Where's he gone?"

"It's none of my business." I rubbed a hand against my chest. "I think I'm officially single. It's just that no one told me."

"You're not. Neither of you has broken things off. Rhett just needs some space. You can be a bit of a handful."

"So can he! And I did nothing wrong."

Tilly arched a brow. "You investigated a member of his gang as a suspect in a murder."

"Rhett's got issues when it comes to protecting his gang."

"It's what he has to do, being their boss."

I narrowed my eyes at her. "Anyone would think you're on his side."

"It's not about sides. I just don't want to see you unhappy, and Rhett makes you happy. Maybe you could hold out an olive branch."

"Or he could. I was only doing my job. I didn't want to tread on his toes, but I couldn't ignore the fact he was protecting a potential murderer."

"But he wasn't. And you found out who really did it."

"Rhett still lied to me." I waved a hand in the air. "As I said, I'm not thinking about him. He's not in the village, and I'm busy trying to protect our shifters from Kirk the Jerk."

Tilly chuckled. "Fair enough. But I'm here if you want to talk about him, and I'll try to be as impartial as possible." She leaned back in her seat. "How are Aurora and Lex getting on? All settled into married life?"

"I guess so. I mean, I've barely seen them since they got married. Lex whisked Aurora off on that amazing honeymoon that he kept extending. They were supposed to be away for two weeks and didn't return for almost two months. And now they're away again."

Tilly sighed. "It must be wonderful to have someone spoil you like that. Is Aurora happy?"

"Blissfully happy. When I have seen her, she keeps telling me I need to get married, and it's the best thing she's ever done. Talk about rubbing salt in the wounds."

"Aurora only wants to see you happy with Rhett. I'm glad it's worked out for her. Your sister had a rocky relationship start."

"I know. She does deserve this. I just wish Lex wouldn't keep taking her away all the time."

"You sound jealous," Tilly said.

I shrugged. "A bit. I've been used to it being the two of us for a long time. Not that I have any problems with Lex, but I miss not having Aurora around."

"Give her time. They're still in the newly married phase. Sadly, the glow fades after a while."

I didn't like to admit it, but I did feel lonely. I'd come to rely on Aurora too much, and now I didn't have her, and with Rhett out of the picture, I didn't have many other places to turn to.

Tilly squeezed my arm. "You know where I am if ever you need cake and a chat."

"You're always busy here. I don't want to get in the way."

"Bother me all you like. I can handle a busy restaurant and chat to my friend. And I'll keep my ear to the ground to see if I hear anything about who's going around biting women."

"Thanks. Any information could be useful." I glanced over at the tempting display of cakes and pastries and licked my lips. "I'll take a couple more slices of that cake to go. If I don't get some for Wiggles, he won't speak to me for a week."

"Coming right up." Tilly boxed up the cake, and I paid for the food and drinks before heading out.

"There'd better be something in that box for me," Wiggles said. "I've been bored rigid waiting out here."

"There is. And it's worth the wait. Let's eat cake then check in with the angels, see what evidence they found on Sabine's body that could lead us to our killer."

"Definitely cake first," Wiggles said.

I flipped open the lid. "Of course. We must get our priorities right."

Chapter 10

After we'd eaten Tilly's amazing red velvet cake, and Wiggles had thoroughly investigated the box for crumbs, we headed into Angel Force.

Cassiel was on the front desk and greeted me with her usual surly expression.

"How's the investigation going with Sabine?" I asked.

She handed me a visitor's badge and made me sign in. She always did things by the book. "I've looked over the body."

"And..."

Cassiel sighed. "This way. I'll show you what I found."

I hid a grin. She was the grumpiest angel I'd ever met.

"Do you want to take a look at the body?"

I shook my head. "Nope. I'm sure you did a great investigation of the corpse. I wouldn't mind taking a look at the report, though."

Dazielle walked over as Cassiel strode off to grab the paperwork, a sullen look on her face. "Give me an update. What have you found out?"

It was a good job I was in such a positive mood thanks to Tilly's cake, or I might have snapped back.

"I've been talking to a few people who knew Sabine. So far, no one's had a bad word to say about her. I've ruled out Kirk Wrangler, unfortunately. I was sure it was him, but he was eating dinner in Tilly's restaurant when Sabine was bitten."

"The bite marks aren't so important to this investigation. We've had an interesting twist from our end," Dazielle said.

"What's the twist?" From the smug look on her face, she was enjoying keeping me in the dark.

"The bite didn't kill Sabine."

"Oh! So what killed her?" I said.

Cassiel returned and handed me the file. "It was a stab wound in her neck. The knife hit a vein, and she bled out."

"I didn't see a stab wound when I found Sabine." I looked over the file, flicking through the pictures quickly. Even just seeing a photo of all that blood made my stomach turn.

"The bite marks concealed the stab wound," Cassiel said. "It was only when I took a closer look that I found the mortal wound."

"That makes sense. What kind of weapon was used to stab her?" I said.

"Possibly a curved knife or a talon."

"A talon? So it could have been a magic using creature? A bird shifter? But we don't have any of those around here."

"That's a funny thing about bird shifters, they have these things called wings." Cassiel smirked at me. "The killer may not be from around here."

I ignored her jab. She had a point, but she didn't need to be so mean in making it.

"If it was a knife, it could have been anyone," Dazielle said. "And I know your Uncle Kenny only has weak magic. He could have used a blade to kill Sabine."

"And done what with the bloody murder weapon? I found him. He had no blade in his hand. Did you find a knife when you searched the area?"

"No, but that doesn't mean he didn't stash it somewhere."

"And he is a member of your family," Cassiel said. "Maybe you helped him hide it so he wouldn't get in trouble."

"Get that thought out of your head," I said. "I'll stake my life on Uncle Kenny being innocent."

"So, he was just in the wrong place at the wrong time?" Dazielle said.

"Exactly that. And he has an alibi."

"Which we know your Auntie Queenie faked," Dazielle said. "I'm within my rights to arrest them both. It's a crime to lie to the angels."

"Then you should probably arrest me too," I muttered.

"Been there, done that," Dazielle said.

I snorted a laugh. "You can't seriously still have Uncle Kenny as a suspect?"

"And you can't be neutral over his involvement. He hasn't given me a proper answer as to what he was doing in the woods."

I lifted a shoulder. I didn't want to reveal Basil to Dazielle. She'd jump on him as the killer, and I had him down as just another gentle soul who didn't need persecution. Although I wasn't removing him from my private suspect list yet.

"Uncle Kenny likes to take walks in the evening. And he was worried about the crowds in the woods, disturbing the animals. He's not who you need to focus on. What else can you tell me about Sabine's murder?"

Dazielle glanced at Cassiel, who lifted her chin and sighed. She hated helping me.

"The bite mark on Sabine's body happened before she was stabbed," Cassiel said. "It could be two attackers."

"A biter and a stabber?" I said.

"Kenny could be working with a shifter to commit murder," Dazielle said.

"It's not even the tiniest bit funny that you're still saying his name."

She lifted her hands. "It does appear that Sabine was bitten and then stabbed."

"Sabine was bitten to incapacitate her, or kill her, but it failed, so she had to be stabbed. But why were the other bite victims not stabbed? What was different about Sabine?"

"We can't find anything unusual about her," Cassiel said.

"She's got no criminal record," Dazielle said. "Sabine lived a quiet life."

"And she was definitely human?" I said. "There was nothing magic on her body?"

"What kind of magic are you talking about?" Dazielle said.

"I had a chat with Bella, her best friend. She said, when they were kids, they had imaginary friends.

She called them pixies, and Sabine introduced Bella to them."

"Bella could see the pixies too?"

"No, she never saw them, but she said Sabine took them seriously. Is it possible Sabine had magic?"

"Nothing showed on my tests," Cassiel said. "But there are some humans with mild magic abilities. They never become aware of them because they have no education."

"Run your tests again. Sabine was interested in magic artifacts. Perhaps she had an idea she was different but didn't know what it was. She could even have taken the job with Kirk to see if she could learn more."

"You think her magic ability got her killed?" Dazielle said.

"Not everyone likes people who use magic, Kirk being one of them. He has a real thing against shifters. I just wish he didn't have such a good alibi."

"I've done all the tests I need to do," Cassiel said. "I didn't miss anything. Sabine didn't use magic."

I looked at Dazielle for support. She shrugged but then nodded.

"Check the tests again," she said to Cassiel, "just to be sure. I assumed Sabine was human, but if her magic was suppressed, or she didn't know she was able to use it, it could be so weak that it wasn't detected."

"It's a waste of time, but if you insist, I'll take another look." Cassiel snatched the file from my hand and marched away.

"You won't be in her good books for questioning her ability to do her job," Dazielle said.

"I wasn't. Cassiel's great when it comes to corpses. Besides, I've never been in her good books. She doesn't like me."

Dazielle grunted. "Even if we learn Sabine had magic, that doesn't put your Uncle Kenny in the clear. He was hiding something when I interviewed him."

I frowned. So Dazielle hadn't missed my uncle's poor effort at hiding the truth. I needed to find the killer before she learned about Basil and Uncle Kenny's attempts at keeping him hidden.

"I'm going to speak to Oakley next. He has to be on the suspect list. He dated Sabine, and she ditched him. Maybe there was unfinished business between them. He could have come here to talk to Sabine and things went wrong," I said.

"It's worth investigating. I need to speak to Tate."

"About what? Free pizza for the angels?"

"Someone reported seeing him with Sabine the day she died."

"Tate would have seen lots of people that day. He runs the most popular pizza parlor in the village." I didn't like where Dazielle was heading with this line of investigation.

"Tempest! He's a werewolf."

I groaned. She was so predictable. "You saw the bite marks on Sabine. There's no way a shifter did that. Besides, Tate was with me and Wiggles that night. We were running interference to keep the shifters safe."

"You were together all evening?" Dazielle said.

"No! But that doesn't mean Tate attacked Sabine. Wiggles wasn't around the whole time. You'll be accusing him next."

"I could, but there was no lingering smell of hellhound on the body. I can always tell when Wiggles has been around." Her gaze shifted to my furry little friend as he squirmed out from under a desk with something hanging out of his mouth. "Do you have evidence to show where Tate was when Sabine was stabbed?"

"I... Well, technically, no. But I can't account for most of the villagers at that time. That doesn't make them guilty of anything."

"Tate could have shifted. It was almost a full moon that night. He lost control of his wolf and attacked Sabine. He would have been able to get away before you discovered him."

"Sure, but getting back to the bite marks, those weren't made by a shifter."

"Tate only partially shifted. Some werewolves can do that."

"And stabbed her too? Nope, I'm not buying any of this. Tate isn't involved."

"I still need to discount him. You focus on Oakley, and I'll question Tate."

I shook my head. This would go badly. Tate was always helping people, but when it was a full moon, he had a short fuse. Mild mannered Tate could turn into snappy, growling Tate if you weren't careful. And if Dazielle blundered in and pointed the finger at him, he'd soon be snarling.

"Do you have a problem with my plan?" Dazielle said. "Or would you rather I focus on your Uncle Kenny?"

"No, fine. You talk to Tate, but I'll back him up on this. And you're still missing the fact the bite didn't kill Sabine. A knife did."

"I'm covering all bases," Dazielle said. "Shifters can have trouble controlling their inner beasts. If nothing else, I'm discounting him as a suspect."

"Discount him in a nice way," I said. "Tate's a good guy. So is Uncle Kenny."

"If you're so certain they're not involved, you should be helping to find out who did this." Dazielle leaned forward and brushed cake crumbs off my shirt. "Not hanging out with Wiggles and eating."

I glowered at her, biting my tongue so I didn't say something I'd regret. She was in a terrible mood. Even if I'd agreed with everything she'd just said, she still wouldn't be happy.

"I will. I'll make sure Uncle Kenny and Tate are in the clear."

"Good luck with that. And find me my killer."

I hurried away before I got another tongue lashing or decided to see how much damage I could do to Dazielle before her angel buddies came to her rescue.

It was time to speak to my next suspect.

Chapter 11

"You should all be burned at the stake. I don't trust any of you. Which one of you killed Sabine?"

I glanced at Wiggles. We'd only been in the village for ten minutes, looking for Oakley. "That sounds like our next suspect. What's up with him?"

"Let's go check it out," Wiggles said.

We sped up and turned the corner. There was a small crowd gathered around Oakley. He had a bottle in his hand and was waving it around as he staggered about.

"This place is weird," he yelled. "Why do you let dangerous animals roam about in your woods? And you're all strange, too. Don't think I don't see the odd stuff that goes on around here."

The crowd grumbled their unhappiness. They were mainly residents, and none of them enjoyed being called weird or odd or having the village disrespected.

"I'm getting the real police here. The ones in Willow Tree Falls are bizarre. Why do they dress all in white? And why are they tall, pretty, and blonde? Do they have something against short, ugly people?"

I pushed through the crowd and strode toward Oakley. "You need to calm down."

"Who are you to tell me to calm down? My girlfriend's dead, and no one is doing anything about it." He swung around and staggered toward me. His blond hair looked like it hadn't been brushed, and his face was puffy from where he'd been crying.

"Oakley, I was with Sabine in the marquee when you arrived in the village. And I promise you, her death is being investigated. I'm helping to figure out what happened to her."

"You can't be helping. You look nothing like the rest of the weirdo police around here. You're too short, too pale, and your hair is the wrong color. And you're wearing mostly black. They wouldn't let you through the door."

"I work freelance. They let pale, non-blondes do that kind of work," I said. "Don't you remember meeting me when you first got to the village?"

His bleary gaze met mine. "Oh, yeah. Okay, maybe I have seen you before."

"That's right. I'm Tempest."

"Oakley Bannister. I'm... I mean, I was Sabine's friend. Sorry, I didn't recognize you at first. I wasn't paying much attention to anything other than Sabine that day. It had been a while since I'd seen her. Now, I won't see her ever again." He took a drink from his bottle.

"You used to date, didn't you?"

"Yeah, but I was an idiot and let her go. Now it's too late to show her I've changed. We could have been together." A tear trickled down his stubbled chin and dropped to the ground.

I patted his shoulder as I glanced at the watching crowd. "The show's over. Everything's under control."

Puddles Lavern, a local realtor, scurried over on her high heels. "He wasn't being polite. He needs to be careful. Everyone is jumpy at the moment. The angels are poking around and asking questions, and the shifters are scared."

"Angels? Shifters? What's she talking about?" Oakley said.

I glared at her. "Thanks, Puddles. I'll take it from here." We made a point of being careful about not revealing ourselves to non-magic users. Puddles seemed to have forgotten that.

Her cheeks flushed. "He's been drinking. He won't remember this conversation. I'm just telling you what I know. This young man's not being sensible, shouting about burning us at the stake. And given your particular... specialty, Tempest, you should be especially careful when someone makes a threat like that." She tottered away.

"Let's go somewhere quiet," I said to Oakley. "I'd like to talk to you about Sabine."

He looked at the bottle in his hand, and his body crumpled. "I'm not handling this well. I didn't come here to cause trouble. I was excited to see Sabine, but we barely got a chance to talk. And then she was dead."

I eased the bottle from his hand and placed it in a trash can. "Let's go. I'll find you a coffee, and you can sober up."

He grabbed a bag beside his feet and nodded. "Thanks. I didn't mean to upset people, but I'm so angry about what happened."

I looked around for somewhere quiet to go. There were still a few people watching us. "Let's go to the museum. It should be quiet this time of the day."

Oakley shrugged and stumbled along beside me, clutching the bag against his chest.

I pushed open the door to the Museum of Magic and Witchcraft and stepped inside its cool, quiet interior. There were a few tourists wandering around, but we had the place almost to ourselves.

I bought Oakley a coffee from the vending machine and handed it to him.

He took several sips as his gaze moved around the main hall. "What kind of museum is this?"

"Well, since you were yelling about burning people at stakes and how weird this place is, I figured you needed an introduction to witchcraft and magic."

"It's a witch museum?" His eyes narrowed.

"Something like that. It's interesting. You don't have to believe in it to take a look. And you never know, you might even learn something. This way. We'll check out the witches first." Unlike Kirk's marquee exhibits, everything here had been gifted to the museum.

He trudged along behind me, sipping his coffee. "It's like this place has no choice but to be weird. Everyone's all spiritual and spooky."

"It's not so weird, but you're right about the village being different to most places. We have an ancient stone circle and a thermal spa that people say helps restore their health."

"Nah, it's way more than that," Oakley said. "I keep seeing flashes of weird things, but when I look, they're gone."

I stopped by a display of witch stones. "What kind of weird are we talking about?"

"One of your pretty police officers had wings. I saw these enormous white wings behind her, and then they were gone. And there was this other guy, he came out from under a bridge. He was huge, green, and kind of warty. He saw me, and the next time I blinked, he was a normal guy scrambling up the rocks. I asked him about it, but he laughed as if he didn't know what I was talking about."

It sounded like Oakley had untapped magic running through his veins. Only people with magic could see our unique residents.

"This museum is all about the history of Willow Tree Falls. It's a special place."

"A place where you have to believe in magic to live here?"

"Why not? Are you prepared to believe magic could be real since you've seen wings where they shouldn't be?"

He shrugged. "I don't know. It seems a bit out there for my liking. Although Sabine always felt... otherworldly. It's the only way I can describe her. I sometimes thought she might simply vanish on the breeze."

"Vanish on the breeze?" Oakley must have had more to drink than I'd realized. "What was she going to do, fly away?"

"I hoped she'd stay with me forever. There was something different about her, and she was really into magic. She was always dragging me to places that were supposed to be mystical and full of energy. I used to tease her that she was a tree hugger, you know, communing with nature and talking to the animals. She'd just smile and agree with me, like it was no big deal."

"Did you ever see Sabine doing anything odd?"

Oakley glanced at me. "Odd how?"

"Well, do something you'd consider to be magic."

"Yeah, sure. Spells aren't real."

"And the wings and the troll guy from under the bridge were tricks of the light?"

"Um, maybe." Oakley swallowed and glanced around the quiet room. "You're not secretly a witch and planning on cursing me for getting drunk and making an idiot of myself in your village?"

I smiled. "I do love the place I live in, so it's not nice when someone disrespects it and the people who live here, but you're safe for now. I promise, no curses."

He chuckled. "Sorry, that was a dumb thing to say. You're not a witch, not if you're trying to figure out what happened to Sabine. She was my better half. She used to nudge me when I got lazy. I wish I'd been different. I'd still have Sabine. Maybe she'd still be alive. I never wanted her to split up with me."

"You wanted her back?" I said.

Oakley stopped in front of a display of wands. "I loved her. I was hoping we could sort things out, and she'd marry me. I've never cared about anyone like I did Sabine. I had girlfriends before her, but none were serious. When I met her, it was so different. We fit together like missing pieces of a puzzle. Then I got complacent and let things slide, so she got rid of me. I only have myself to blame, but I was turning things around. I got a job and was saving money. I wanted Sabine to be proud of me. Now, I've lost the chance to win her back."

"I'm sorry you lost her," I said. "I didn't know her well, but she seemed nice."

"Sabine was the best. She loved all this magic stuff. I used to worry about her, because she was always going on adventures to find remote places or weird items that were supposed to have magic in them."

After hearing that, I was willing to bet my next dozen triple chocolate brownies that Sabine had some magic ability, even if Cassiel hadn't discovered it through her tests.

"What did she like to investigate?" I asked.

"Anything, as long as it was weird and unexplainable. Sabine once told me she could see weird little creatures at the bottom of the garden. She even talked to them when she was a kid. I figured she was joking, but she seemed serious. And she used to collect jewelry that was supposed to have magical properties. She wore it all the time."

Jewelry was an excellent way to store magic. It could be used discreetly without anyone else seeing what you were up to.

"Did Sabine like particular stones or gems?" I said.

"No, and some of the stuff wasn't pretty, but she said it made her feel good. She'd pick up stones and drill holes in them to wear as necklaces. She said they connected her to the environment. I didn't say much about it, so long as it kept her happy."

"Did you talk to Sabine before she died and tell her how you felt?" I guided Oakley to the next display, which was full of potion bottles.

"She must have known I liked her, although I didn't come right out and say it. We were planning to meet up after she'd finished work. She was late, so we went looking for her. I'd planned on asking to meet up alone the next day to see if we could figure things out. I wanted to show her everything I'd done to see if I could get her to change her mind and come back to me."

Was Oakley telling the truth, or had he actually met Sabine that night? They'd fought and things had gone wrong. This could be a crime of passion.

"Were you with Bella when you learned what happened to Sabine?" I said.

He scrubbed his forehead. "That's right. And we were getting worried about Sabine when she didn't show."

"Do you spend a lot of time with Bella?"

"Yeah, she's a mate."

"Is there anything going on with you two?"

He grinned and shook his head. "No. People often ask that, and we used to get teased that I was dating both of them because we're all so close. I love Bella. She's like a sister to me. And she was around when I met Sabine. Fortunately, we hit it off. She always had Sabine's back. I like her, but there's nothing going on between us, and there never will be. It would be too weird. Like kissing your sister." He stuck his tongue out.

Oakley's alibi tallied with what Bella told me, which put them in the clear. No crime of passion here.

"Can you think of anyone who had a problem with Sabine?" I said.

He scrubbed at his chin. "I can think of one person. Kirk Wrangler. I can't stand the guy. Sabine had worked with him for about six months. She rarely said anything bad about anyone but didn't have a good word about Kirk. That means he must have been an ogre."

"What didn't she like about him?"

"Kirk exploited her. She'd have found another job, but she felt trapped. She hated Kirk, but loved working with those artifacts. She'd bought into the fact they were special." Oakley turned and pressed his forehead against the glass cabinet. His shoulders shook, and he covered his eyes with one hand. "I spoke to a police officer, and he let slip Sabine's death was more complicated than an animal attack. Do you know anything about that?"

I patted his shoulder. "It's possible it's not so straightforward."

"That's why you're asking me questions?"

"Yes, the police believe it was murder."

Oakley sucked in a shaky breath. "Who did it?"

"We're looking into it. Coming back to Kirk, did he know Sabine didn't like him?"

He stood back and swiped at his eyes. "If he did, he wouldn't have cared. If I'd been with her, maybe I could have convinced her to find another job. This is my fault."

"No, it's not. You couldn't have stopped this. And like you said, Sabine loved coming to places like this. What's to say she wouldn't have come here anyway just to see Kirk's exhibition?"

"Maybe. I don't know much about anything anymore. I feel lost." Oakley wandered to another cabinet and stopped in front of it. "Hey, Sabine had some things like this." He pointed at the amulets in front of him.

"She did?"

"Yeah. In her stuff."

"Amulets can be powerful. They're used to store spells or even curses. And they can act as a source of protection if anyone ever attacks you."

He slid me a glance. "You believe in all that?"

"If Sabine could believe in it, why can't I?"

Oakley stared at the amulets for a moment. "It scares me."

"What does?"

"Magic. I don't want to believe in it, but some of the things Sabine said, it made me wonder. Could there be something to it? Could she see things I'd never understand? She always came alive when she talked about magic. It was her special thing. I was a bit envious. Sabine was so convinced it was real, but I didn't get it."

"Don't be so sure you don't get magic. After all, you reckoned you saw a troll coming out from under a bridge."

He dragged a hand through his messy hair. "Sure I did. Or it was just some weird looking dude, and I need glasses."

I smiled at him. "You said Sabine had amulets like this. Do you know where they are?"

Oakley pulled open the bag he held. "Sure. This is her stuff. I picked it up from the trailer she was staying in." He dug around in the bag and pulled out half a dozen amulets.

I touched one and a zing of magic rocketed up my arm. I jerked my hand back and flexed my fingers. Where had she gotten this? It was buzzing with energy.

"Is something wrong?" Oakley asked.

"No, all good here." My eyes widened as I studied the amulets. These could have come from Kirk's collection. Sabine told him that the amulets had gone missing, but did she steal them? If so, it would have given Kirk a great motive for getting back at her. I imagined he wasn't the kind of guy to let someone steal from him and get away with it.

Oakley looked at the amulets. "They're not her usual style."

"Do you know where they came from?" I brushed a finger lightly over another amulet. Yep, they contained power, far too much power for a human to control.

"No idea. And I don't know what to do with them." Oakley looked into the glass cabinet again. "Maybe this museum could use them in their collection. They'd fit right in."

"This place would be perfect for them. I know the manager, so I'll see if she's interested in displaying them. I can take them now, if you like."

"Sure. Have them. Sabine has no family to pass them on to, and I never saw her wear these, so they're either new, or she didn't like them." Oakley handed them over.

More spiky magic flickered across my skin.

"I'd better go," he said. "I've got a few apologies to make. I didn't mean to offend anyone who lives here."

"Sober up before you make your apologies, but people will understand. You're grieving because you lost someone you loved. That would make any of us do silly things."

"Thanks. I appreciate that." He finished his coffee and left the museum.

"I can feel the magic on those amulets from here," Wiggles said. "What was Sabine doing with loads of powerful magic items?"

"I'm more interested in where she got them from. Did she take them from Kirk and he found out? It would give him a good motive for wanting her dead."

"None of us like Kirk, but he's got an alibi."

I frowned as I tucked the amulets into my jacket pocket. "Which is annoying."

"What do you want to do now?" Wiggles said. "I'm in the mood for more cake. We could go back to Tilly's."

"I need to check out these amulets," I said. "Let's go to the apartment and see if we can figure out what they do."

I'd only taken a few steps away from the museum entrance, when Merrie stormed over.

"That's it. I've had enough. I quit!"

Chapter 12

"Merrie! What's going on? You can't quit." She was my rock at Cloven Hoof. Merrie was always there when I got busy or had to leave the village to demon hunt. I couldn't be without her.

Merrie puffed out her cheeks. "Zandra is being impossible. I can't deal with her. I'm all for giving people second chances, but I'm not sure she deserves one."

"Where is she?"

"At the club. She showed up and messed up everything." Merrie jammed her hands on her hips. "I had to walk out, or I'd have yelled at her."

"Let me handle Zandra." I started walking back to Cloven Hoof. "I'll speak to her again about her role."

"I thought you'd already tried that." Merrie hurried along beside me. "She has to go, or I will."

"Don't quit. I need you. I thought Zandra had listened to me. I sometimes forget she resents the fact—" I bit my tongue. I still wasn't telling everyone about Zandra.

"The fact what?" Merrie jabbed me in the side with a finger. "Is she someone special?"

"Um, I just don't think she likes being told what to do by me."

"Or by anyone," Merrie said. "She keeps trying to take over. We have a system in the club, and it's always worked smoothly."

"It has, and we do. You do an amazing job of keeping it all together. Don't worry. I'll sort this out."

We jogged the rest of the way to Cloven Hoof, and I raced through the doors. My heart lurched into my throat. Zandra stood in front of the bar, her hands raised. There were dozens of full bottles of alcohol floating in the air.

I grabbed Merrie's arm so she wouldn't yell. "Don't say a word. I've seen what happens when Zandra gets distracted when she's doing a spell. Ka-boom!"

Merrie clapped a hand over her mouth, her breath heaving out of her and tears in her eyes. She loved this bar even more than I did.

I continued to watch Zandra as the bottles wobbled slowly onto the shelves. Only when they were back in a safe place did I finally release a breath.

Zandra turned, a triumphant look on her face. "I told you I could do it, Merrie. You don't need to do everything by hand. What's the point of having magic if you don't use it to do boring stuff like this?"

Merrie glared at me. "You said you'd fix this."

"I will. Go take a break."

Merrie glared at Zandra and then stamped into the kitchen, slamming the door behind her.

"What's wrong with her? She's acting like she's my boss," Zandra said. "I was doing her a favor. Look, they're arranged by color."

"Which is pretty, but now some of our popular drinks are on the top shelves. You have to use a ladder to get up there. It's not practical. See those three bottles of red liquid at the top? We refill those at least once a week because they're so popular. You'd have to keep scrabbling up the shelves to grab those."

"Oh! I didn't know that. Merrie never said."

"She arranges the drinks that get requested most often so they're in easy reach. The more eclectic drinks and the stuff we only pull out on special holidays get left on the top shelves. That way, people can see them so they know they're there when they want them."

"Huh! I guess Merrie did mention something about that. She kept talking about the holidays and not to change the order of things. I wasn't paying much attention. I thought the place needed a different look. You don't like it?"

I didn't miss the shimmer of dejection that crossed Zandra's face. "It looks great. But having to work the bar set up like this would be a nightmare."

"I was trying to help." Zandra slumped onto a stool. "I can't get anything right."

"You did well. But stay away from the bar and Merrie for now." I sat next to her. "Maybe you'd like to have a go at security work."

"You mean I can throw people out of this place?" A sharp smile crossed Zandra's face. "Can I use magic to do that?"

"I, um, well, maybe security work isn't for you." I didn't need another murder to deal with if Zandra's power got out of control.

She scowled at me. "I shouldn't even be here. I keep having to hide who I am. Merrie's asked me several ways about how I know you. What am I supposed to tell everyone? Dad's still not figured out how to introduce me to the village or some such rubbish."

I wrapped an arm around her shoulders. "We tell them the truth. There's no reason we should keep you a secret. I just didn't want word getting out before Mom was ready."

"Dad hasn't exactly been telling everyone about me. It goes to show he doesn't want me around."

"Of course he does. You know the reasons he's being cautious. But my staff are discreet, and they won't gossip. Stay here while I get Merrie." I wasn't sure I was doing the right thing, but I was done hiding my half-sister from people. And Dad wasn't doing enough to look out for her. I understood he had to have a careful balance between his two lives, but sometimes you have to shove things off balance to get any forward motion.

Merrie was sitting at the table in the kitchen, sipping an herbal tea. "Is my bar back the way it should be?"

"Not yet. We'll deal with that in a minute, and Zandra won't interfere with the bar any more until we both feel she's ready. Come on. I've got something to tell you."

Merrie set down her mug and followed me into the bar.

I walked back to Zandra and put my arm around her shoulders again. "Merrie, I haven't introduced you to Zandra."

Merrie's brow wrinkled. "You have. You introduced us the other day."

"You don't know who she is, though. She's my half-sister."

Merrie's jaw dropped. "Wow! Of course. I see the resemblance. Why didn't you tell me you were related? And how? I don't get it."

"Our dad is too scared to tread on people's toes," Zandra muttered.

I gave her a squeeze. "But I'm not. It's one of the reasons I want her here. Zandra was looking for work, so I helped out. And you were complaining we're short-staffed."

Merrie's gaze ran over Zandra. "I see you can do magic, and there's power behind it. It makes sense now I know you're a Crypt witch."

"I'm not. I mean, Dad's not got much power," Zandra said. "I don't know where it comes from."

"You're still family. You are a Crypt witch. You're one of us," I said. "And Zandra tried an age spell on herself, which is why she looks so old. She's really eight."

"No! I'm eighteen. I'm not a kid."

"Wow! This is a lot. And what you blast out is intense, Zandra. I don't want you doing magic around my bar," Merrie said.

"Your bar?" Zandra said. "Tempest owns this place."

"I do own the bar. But without Merrie, Cloven Hoof would be nothing. She keeps everything together. She's my right-hand woman in this place, and you need to respect that. If she says you're not ready for the bar, then don't interfere."

"I already told you I was just trying to help," Zandra said.

"Help when Merrie asks, but don't take over," I said.

"Maybe I can do a better job than her," Zandra said.

Merrie laughed. "Oh, yeah, Zandra is definitely like you. You're stubborn and always think you're right."

"We're not stubborn," I said at the same time as Zandra.

I laughed, and Zandra smiled.

"So, all clear?" I said to her. "This is Merrie's bar. Keep your magical mitts off unless she says otherwise."

"What am I supposed to do if I can't do bar work?"

"Let's go to the office, and we'll figure things out." I let Zandra go on ahead and stopped next to Merrie. "Sorry I didn't tell you sooner about our relationship. I can't give up on her, though. She's had a rough start."

Merrie waved a hand in the air. "Don't say another word. I'll be fine now I know what I'm working with. Of course, she'll be bull-headed and want to do things her own way. She's like you, and I know how to handle you so my wonderful bar doesn't get destroyed."

"I'm not sure if that was an insult." I squeezed her shoulder. "And you're not quitting on me?"

"I'm not." Merrie laughed. "Go look after your sister. I have a bar to set right."

I headed into the office to find Zandra in my seat. "Out. No one sits there but me."

She twirled in the seat then stood and moved to the other side of the desk.

"Now I've started telling people about you, we have to get Dad involved. It's time to let everyone know you're here," I said. "And he still needs to know about your surprise growth spurt."

"I'm not sure that's a good idea." The grin on Zandra's face faded as she perched on the edge of another seat.

"Why not?"

"What if the rest of your family don't like me?"

"They'll like you. They'll be surprised you've been here and haven't been to visit, though. You'd better have a good reason."

Zandra looked at the floor. "They won't think I'm good enough. Is that a decent reason?"

"No! Let's get Dad on the snow globe and tell him you're here."

"Can't it wait? We should leave it another few days. I may decide I don't like it here and move on. I don't want to get his hopes up that I'm staying."

"No more stalling." I activated the snow globe and contacted Dad.

"Tempest. How's everything going?" His face appeared in the snow globe.

"Things are... interesting."

"I heard about you working with the angels on that murder in the woods. I hope you're taking care."

"I always take care of business." I looked up at Zandra, and she shook her head. "Zandra's here."

He blinked several times. "In the village? I haven't seen her. How long has she been here?"

Zandra shook her head again.

"Not long. I figured we needed a family dinner, though. Get everyone together so she can feel included."

"Of course. Is she there with you?"

I waved Zandra over, and after scowling, she climbed to her feet and peered over my shoulder. "Hey, Dad. Surprise!"

"Who... Zandra? That can't be you."

"Double surprise. I got big."

His mouth hung open. "Is this a joke?"

"No joke. Zandra's got power. And she decided to grow up fast," I said. "She's been reluctant to let you know."

"I... I'm not surprised. Young lady, we need to talk."

Zandra huffed out a breath. "I knew you wouldn't want to see me."

"It's not that. It's great to see you. You should have dropped by when you arrived. But now I see why you didn't. Can you reverse the spell?"

"No! I've had enough of being a kid. I've been looking after myself for too long."

Dad was quiet for a few seconds. "I'm sorry. I should have been there for you more. But, Zandra, that was a dangerous spell."

"She's handling it," I said. "But I figure Zandra could do with spending time with all of us. With so much power, a steer would be good."

"Tempest offered me a job at Cloven Hoof, so I've been learning the ropes here," Zandra said. "I'm being useful."

"She has? That's good. It sounds like you're planning on sticking around if you're working."

"I don't want to get in your way," she said. "I know you're busy with your family."

"You're my family, too. And you're welcome here as long as you like. Have you got a decent place to stay? Are you good for money?"

"Dad! Quit it. I'm doing okay."

He nodded. "And I'm sure Tempest is looking after you. Let me talk to Cora. We'll sort something out and get you over soon."

"You need her permission before letting me into the house?" The sharp tone in Zandra's voice made me wince.

Dad's warm smile slipped. "It's not like that."

"Hey, don't be mean," I said to Zandra. It hadn't been easy for my mom to accept what Dad had done after he'd gone missing. He'd basically cheated on her, but only because he'd lost his memory and forgotten about his family and his wife. Talk about a sticky situation.

Zandra lifted one shoulder. "Whatever. I won't come if they don't want me to."

"We do. Everyone wants to see you. Give me time to figure something out. And I want to hear about everything you've been doing. It's been too long."

"Sure. I'll see if my new boss can give me time off," Zandra said.

We talked for a few more minutes before saying our goodbyes.

I looked over at Zandra and had to stifle a smile. She reminded me of my younger self, all attitude and sass and quick to take offence if someone said the slightest thing she didn't like. Had I really been that bad? Most likely.

Wiggles punched through the door and bounded into the office. "You need to come outside. There's trouble."

"What's going on?" I said.

"It's Tate. I was out checking his trash behind the pizza parlor when the angels turned up and started causing trouble. There's a fight brewing."

"A fight!" Zandra was on her feet.

"No way. You stay here and keep out of trouble. I'll deal with this," I said.

"But I don't want to miss out on the fun."

"No. You figure out dinner plans with Dad. I'll be right back." I wasn't dragging her into a situation between a werewolf and some powerful angels. "Come on, Wiggles. Let's see what trouble the angels are stirring up."

Chapter 13

I raced out after Wiggles and along the road toward Tate's pizza parlor. He was standing outside the front door, his hands in fists as Dazielle and Dominic stood in front of him. They had their wings fully extended. That was always a bad sign.

"What's going on?" I ran up to them, Wiggles beside me.

"I'm being accused of murder." Tate growled out the words. "Dazielle thinks I killed Sabine."

Several people had stopped to watch the argument, and all murmured as they heard him.

"I didn't say that exactly. Come quietly so we can talk about this at the station. You don't want any trouble," Dazielle said.

"But it seems you do. You just about accused me of murder. I call that one big pile of trouble." Tate glowered at Dazielle. "And once you get me inside Angel Force, you'll shove me in a cell and try to charge me."

"They won't do that." I was almost sure they wouldn't, but Dazielle wasn't thinking all that straight at the moment. First, she'd accused Uncle Kenny of murder, and now she was going after Tate.

It was like she was picking on all the good guys in the village.

"We still need to take your statement," Dazielle said. "Don't make me arrest you."

"Let's take this inside Mystic Mushroom," I said. "Everyone can take a breath, and we'll talk off the record. You're not a suspect in Sabine's murder, Tate."

"I am according to this jumped-up angel," Tate said.

"And I don't do off the record," Dazielle said.

I grabbed her arm. "You can't really believe he's a suspect. I thought you were simply ruling him out."

Dazielle's wings shivered and lowered a fraction. "I have my reasons for questioning him."

"But no evidence. So why don't we keep this calm, grab a slice of pizza, and talk about it inside, where we don't have people watching."

Dazielle glanced around, frowning as she became aware of the onlookers. "Very well. We can do it inside the pizza parlor."

"So long as I let you in," Tate said.

"We really should go inside," Wiggles said. "We don't want the pizza missing us. I can hear a large slice of pepperoni and cheese calling my name."

Tate sighed and shoved the door open. He walked in first, followed by Dazielle and Dominic. Wiggles barged past them and headed for the counter.

I walked in, shut the door, and turned the sign to closed, making a shooing gesture at the people still lurking outside.

"Are we really getting pizza?" Dominic's voice rang with excitement.

"You can have something if you like," Tate said, a grudging note in his voice. "Everything is ready for the evening rush, which means I don't have long. And I won't have my business messed around because you lot have a feather shoved up your—"

"I'm sure this can be done in ten minutes," I said.

"So long as you cooperate," Dazielle said.

"Can I try the smoky bacon and pineapple pizza?" Dominic was examining the menu. "Or maybe the Hawaiian surprise. What's that got on it?"

"More pineapple," I said. "Do you like fruit on your pizza?"

"I don't think I've ever had it before." Dominic grinned at Tate. "Tempest always feeds me pizza when we're on stakeouts."

"No wonder you failed your recent flying exam," Dazielle said. "You're putting on weight."

Dominic's wings slumped.

"Take a seat you two," I said to Dazielle and Dominic. "I'll help Tate get the pizza." I gestured at Tate to head into the kitchen and then turned back to Dazielle. "Quit it with the interrogating. Tate's a good guy. He's helped us in the past."

"Which doesn't mean I'm letting him off the hook if he's involved with what happened to Sabine."

"Why do you think he had anything to do with her murder?"

"Get us some pizza, and I'll tell you," Dazielle said.

I stalked behind the counter and into the kitchen.

Tate was shoveling fresh pizzas out of the oven. He turned and looked at me then shook his head. "You know I had nothing to do with this."

"I do. You were with me for most of the evening."

"Yeah, but I was the one who said we should split up and run diversions. And Dazielle's got a suspicious mind. Maybe she thinks I did it deliberately to give me a chance to get to Sabine."

"You didn't know Sabine, did you?" I ran a pizza cutter through a piping hot triple cheese and smoky bacon pizza.

"No, but I could be lying about that, especially if I'm a dangerous monster who can't be trusted."

"Tate, don't worry. Dazielle's off her game. She's even willing to believe my Uncle Kenny is a suspect. If she can do that, she could pin this on anyone. We'll get this sorted, even if I have to knock her head against the wall to get the sense to return."

"You could be knocking for a long time." He grabbed my elbow and gave it a squeeze. "Thanks, Tempest. I appreciate you being here. Dazielle was getting up in my face and making me angry. My wolf was stirring. And it doesn't help that it's a full moon tonight."

"I'll keep her under control. Let's get this pizza out there and see if that makes her mood improve." We headed back to the main seating area in the pizza parlor with three large pizzas, and Tate dished them up.

We sat around, eating pizza, no one seeming to want to begin the conversation.

After Dazielle had taken about five minutes to chew her first bite of pizza, she set it down and wiped her hands on a napkin. "Tate, you were seen flirting with Sabine."

He jerked back in his seat and lowered his pizza crust to the table. "I was?"

"You talked to her when she came in here on the evening of her murder."

"Err, okay, but I talk to a lot of people. I have to when they order food. Why do you think I was flirting with her?" Tate glanced at me.

"She was an attractive woman, she was single, and you're... you." Dazielle waved a hand at Tate.

"What are you suggesting about Tate?" I said.

"He's a passably attractive man with no commitments. It's only natural he flirted with Sabine."

Had she lost her mind? That was her reason for thinking Tate was involved in this?

"If no one overheard the conversation Tate had with Sabine, it could have been as simple as a pizza order," I said. "And Tate's a friendly guy. He always chats to his customers."

"I sure am. But I can check if Sabine came in and what she ordered. I keep records so I know what's popular." Tate jumped up and headed behind the counter, returning with a notepad. He flicked through several pages. "Here it is. I remember this order now. Sabine got sent in with a long list of dinner requests for everyone working at the marquee."

"You don't remember Sabine? My witness is certain you flirted with her," Dazielle said.

"She didn't stick in my head. I took the order and got to work. That was it."

"Did you find her attractive?" Dazielle said.

"I'd say no, since he can't even remember her," I said.

"Let Tate speak," Dazielle said.

"Sorry, I don't remember Sabine. And I didn't pursue her or attack her in the woods. I'm not that kind of guy."

"Did your wolf have an interest in her?" Dazielle said. "The moon phase would make him strong. He could have seen something he liked, taken control, and gone after Sabine."

Dominic was munching on his pizza, watching the questioning like it was a scene from his favorite movie.

"No way. I always have a handle on my wolf, and I know what he does. Our link is strong. He paid no attention to Sabine."

"He didn't consider her his soulmate?" Dazielle said. "Or decide to hunt her that night and take a bite to see how she tasted?"

Tate scrunched up his face. "No, and when we meet our soulmate, we'll both know. It would be impossible for my wolf to be interested in a woman without me knowing."

"Unless you don't have such good control over your wolf. It's nothing to be ashamed of if you're struggling and need help." Dazielle's gaze shifted to me. "There are other magic users around here who struggle to control their darker sides."

I ignored the jab in my direction. "I've already told you, Tate was with me and Wiggles that night."

"And you also informed me that you split up. That gave him an opportunity," Dazielle said.

Dominic reached for another slice of pizza, but Dazielle slapped the back of his hand.

"Tate had no motive for killing Sabine," I said.

"We only have his word for that," Dazielle said.

"I was with him," Wiggles said around a mouthful of pizza.

Dazielle glared at Wiggles. "The whole time?"

"Most of it. I lost sight of him for about thirty seconds. We were watching each other through the trees while spooking the hunters. Tate did nothing wrong. He raced around and made some impressive howling noises to get the tourists stirred up. It was great. But he didn't kill anyone."

"You lost sight of him for some of the time?" Dazielle shifted in her seat. "He could have attacked Sabine then."

"I only lost sight of him now and again. And I'd have known if Tate shifted into a werewolf. They smell of damp, moldy fur. It's gross."

"Thanks a lot, Wiggles," Tate said.

"You get used to it, but I'd recognize that stench anywhere, and it wasn't in the woods that night. There were no werewolves out while we were messing with the hunters."

Dazielle shifted her attention back to Tate, her eyes narrowing. "Can you confirm that you're able to shift partially? You can be part-man and part-wolf?"

Tate grimaced. "I can, but it hurts like anything, so I avoid doing it. I can do a complete shift easily, there's just a brief flash of pain and it's over. If I'm partially shifted, I feel the change inching over me. It's agony."

"That's why you didn't smell him, Wiggles," Dazielle said. "If Tate was only partially shifted, the smell would have been less pungent."

"Give up on making me the guilty party." Tate slung down the slice of pizza he'd grabbed. "Instead of trying to pin this murder on me, I'm more interested in Kirk Wrangler."

"For Sabine's murder?" I said.

"He has an alibi," Dazielle said.

"Not for the murder, but I want to know how he has all this information about Willow Tree Falls and our shifters. He should have no clue about this place or our forest dwellers."

"It's a good point," I said. "Kirk has way too much information about us. He's a threat, even if he's not a killer."

"It's not relevant," Dazielle said.

"Keeping this village safe isn't a part of your job?" I arched an eyebrow.

Tate nodded. "Why aren't you chasing him and asking him about where this information is coming from?"

Dazielle stared at him and then blinked rapidly. "I assumed he was guessing. He picked quirky out of the way places with ancient ruins and assumed there was something magical about them."

"It's not guesswork. Kirk knows too much for it to be a coincidence that he's here," I said. "And he has accurate illustrations of shifters and knows how to kill them. You don't find that kind of information without an inside source."

"Maybe he reads my blog," Dominic said.

We shifted our attention to him.

"You have a blog?" I said.

"I do. It's my hobby. It's been running for a few months. I get thousands of hits on it."

"Exactly what do you put on this blog?" Dazielle said.

"Fun stuff. Information about magic. I mainly focus on magical hotspots. That's the content that gets the most hits. I get loads of people asking me questions, too. It's great."

"Do you know who these people are?" Dazielle's expression turned thunderous.

"Most of them have strange usernames, so I don't know much about them. But I get regular contact from several people." Dominic swiped a slice of pizza. "There was one guy asking all about shifters. He was really into it."

"Did he ask you how you kill a shifter?" I leaned forward in my seat.

"Sure. We covered all kinds of topics. He was a magic geek. I enjoyed talking to him, well, typing to him. He said I was clever and appreciated my work."

Dazielle laid her hands flat on the table. "You've been leaking information to non-magic users about us. Sharing secrets you had no right to give out. Do you realize what you've done?"

Dominic swallowed his mouthful of pizza. "It's just fun. No one takes it seriously. Most humans don't believe in magic."

I winced. Dominic had just landed in a heap of trouble if the glare Dazielle gave him was an indication of the angel-like storm about to rain down on his head.

"Dominic, could this person have been Kirk?" I said as gently as I could. "What if he was pumping you for information so he could come after our shifters?"

His face paled and the hand holding his pizza shook. "I didn't think. There's no harm in what I was doing."

"There's a lot of harm in it. This is a new level of stupidity, even for you," Dazielle said.

"Dominic didn't do this deliberately. It wasn't as if he was being paid to sell our secrets." I glanced at him. "You don't take money for your blog, do you?"

"No! I gave away the information freely. I like talking about our village and how incredible the magic is." He swallowed. "I... I didn't think I was doing anything wrong."

"We'll deal with this later," Dazielle said. "We need to focus on Sabine's murder for now."

I bit my bottom lip. Poor Dominic, but it was dumb of him to blab all over the internet about our secrets. I had no clue how he'd done it. Hardly anyone had a computer in Willow Tree Falls because the components got fried by magic.

Dominic slumped in his seat, and his gaze went to the window.

"So, you have a motive when it comes to Sabine," Dazielle said to Tate.

He scowled at her and sighed. "Remind me what my motive is again?"

"You were interested in her and she turned you down. You didn't like it."

"Just because you think I turn into a bloodthirsty monster when there's a full moon, that doesn't make it true," Tate said. "I can control myself. And I don't mind being rejected. You win some, you lose some when it comes to women. Not that I ever flirted with Sabine."

"So you say," Dazielle said. "But you have a dubious alibi."

"There's nothing dubious about me," Wiggles said. "And I'm his alibi."

Dazielle simply glared at him. "Tate, you have a less than perfect alibi and a motive."

Tate threw up his hands. "Stop picking on me. You should talk to the guy she was with if you're looking for a wronged boyfriend motive."

"She's not seeing anyone," I said.

"Sabine was with some guy when she made the pizza order. I remember him now you jogged my memory. He knocked over a load of ketchup bottles. He was tall, with messy blond hair."

"That sounds like her ex-boyfriend, Oakley," I said.

"I didn't get his name, but they were having an intense conversation. Sabine wasn't happy. She grabbed the order and left, leaving him here."

"I met Oakley before Sabine was killed," I said. "And I've spoken to him since then. He's got an alibi. I've checked it out."

Tate shrugged. "I can only tell you what I saw. Things weren't going well between them. You should recheck that alibi."

"And I think we should bring you in for testing," Dazielle said.

"Testing? What do you want to test me for?" Tate said.

"The stability of your wolf. Older werewolves have trouble with control. I have to make sure you're not a threat to the village."

Tate slammed his fists on the table. "I've done nothing wrong."

"Cool it," I muttered.

"No way! Dazielle is after me, and I can't figure out what her problem is. I never break the rules, and I always give you guys free pizza when you come in. We look out for each other. At least, I thought we did."

"Maybe your nice guy image is an act," Dazielle said. "We'll arrange a time for you to come to Angel Force and undergo the tests."

"I'm not being tested. I'm fine," Tate snapped.

"Why are you so focused on these tests?" I said.

"It's the new directive," Dominic muttered.

"Directive about what?"

"The Magic Council has had a few incidents with shifters. We must make sure we don't have anyone dangerous in the village. Since we now have a murder linked to a shifter on our hands, it's my job to make sure everyone remains safe," Dazielle said.

I groaned. She wasn't letting this go. "The murder wasn't done by Uncle Kenny, Tate, or any other shifter."

"Or a Bigfoot," Wiggle said.

I sucked in a breath and shook my head at him. We were still keeping Basil a secret.

Dazielle turned her head slowly to stare at him. "A Bigfoot?"

Wiggles' tail lowered as he glanced at me. "Oh, I mean, I was just thinking. It could have been a Bigfoot or any hairy creature. Or how about a unicorn? They can be mean if you get them out of their hay too early. Yeah, a unicorn. You should look at the unicorns."

"Is there anything you'd like to add to that ramble, Tempest? A Bigfoot would match the description that's been given by the bite victims," Dazielle said.

I played with my piece of pizza. The Bigfoot really was out of the bag. It was time to come clean about Basil. "Don't jump to the wrong conclusion, but we do have a Bigfoot in the woods."

Color rose up Dazielle's cheeks. "You've been withholding information. You know the killer?"

"Basil didn't kill Sabine."

"Basil the Bigfoot?" Dazielle rose slowly, an imposing figure as her wings fluttered out behind her. "Tell me where this creature is?"

"Not a chance. The mood you're in, you'll arrest him."

"I'll arrest you if you don't tell me his location."

I stood and glared up at her. "You're not having him. Give me time to figure this out. I'll find out who killed Sabine, but you won't help if you're charging around arresting innocent people."

"No! I've had enough of your meddling on this case. You're out of here."

I took a step back. "You're taking me off this case?"

"I have no choice. You've been hiding the killer."

"I haven't. I kept quiet about Basil because I knew this was how you'd react."

Dazielle jabbed a finger at me, her wings shaking. "I've heard enough from you. Let's go, Dominic. We have a Bigfoot to hunt down."

"Dazielle, wait! You'll only scare him if you hound him."

"I don't care if I scare him. I need to make sure he doesn't kill anyone else." She grabbed Dominic's arm and dragged him away.

Dominic shot me an apologetic look as he headed out the door.

I dropped back in my seat and thumped my head back against the wall.

Tate touched my arm. "Thanks for having my back and sticking up for me."

"Anytime. Dazielle has a real problem with this case, and it's making her behave like an idiot."

"I noticed that. Have we really got a Bigfoot in the village?" Tate grinned. "That's cool."

"We have, and he is. I've met him. And I don't think Basil killed Sabine, but I need to find a way to get Dazielle to believe that." And that would be difficult with an irate angel on my hands and no way to get access to information on the investigation now I'd been booted off the case.

It didn't matter. I'd solve this problem without the help of the angels.

Chapter 14

"What's the plan?" Tate said as he cleared up the remains of the food.

I paced around the pizza parlor. "I need to stop Basil from being captured."

"I'd offer to help, but I should stay out of this. Dazielle's after me for some reason."

"Probably because of those dumb sounding new regulations she's been issued," I said. "You're good. You stay here. It's best you don't go into the woods. It'll only give Dazielle more ammunition against you. Although now she's fixated on Basil, she may forget you're a suspect."

"Let me know if there's anything I can do to help that won't get me arrested," Tate said.

"Thanks. We'd better get out of here. Come on, Wiggles." I left Mystic Mushroom and headed to Mom's house. I knocked on the door and walked inside. "Is anyone home?"

No one replied. I poked my head into the garden and then jogged up the stairs. The place was empty.

"We could do with Uncle Kenny's help," I said. "I'm not sure Basil will talk to me without him being there."

I scribbled a note and left it on the table, hoping a family member would see it and pass it on to Uncle Kenny in time, then headed off to the woods with Wiggles. "Let's see if we can find our introverted Bigfoot and warn him the angels are after him."

"I feel responsible," Wiggles said.

"For what?"

"Dropping Basil in it. I forgot he was a secret. I got distracted by all the delicious pizza."

"Dazielle would have found out eventually. And if we'd kept it from her for much longer, she'd have only been angrier."

"If that's possible. She's a proper grump at the moment."

"She's always sharp with me."

"Sure, but I mean, she's even grumpier than usual."

"Yeah, something does seem off with Dazielle. Maybe the stress of the job is getting to her."

We kept up a brisk pace and were soon in the area where Basil's hideout was located.

"Are you sure we're going in the right direction?" Wiggles wriggled through a gap behind me. "I don't recognize this path."

"That's because it's not a path. It's just muddy and very green." I stopped and peered around. Everything looked the same but also different. That was the trouble with magical woods. Things moved when they weren't supposed to. "Can you pick up Basil's scent?"

"No. It's nose overload in this place," Wiggles said. "I can smell all sorts of interesting creatures that have scurried past. I've got tree rat, rabbit, werewolf, and cat. That last one stinks."

"What about our scent trails? Can you find them from the last time we were here?"

"Give me a few minutes to sniff around. I'll see what I can find." Wiggles shoved his nose to the ground and began to snuffle.

I took a seat on a tree stump as I waited for his nose to work its magic and looked about, hoping to get my bearings. I still couldn't believe Dazielle had chucked me off this case. Something was rattling her. When this was all over, and if she was speaking to me, I'd see if anything was wrong. A grumpy angel with an attitude was no fun to work with.

A distant moaning drifted toward me. I tilted my head, trying to figure out which direction it had come from.

There was a faint whoop and another groan.

I stood and took a few steps in one direction then another. What was making those noises?

Wiggles reappeared. "I'm onto something."

"Did you pick up our scent trails?"

"No, but I found another scent. Fallon's been here recently."

"That's not good. I just heard some creature groaning. We'd better go see if Fallon's caught something she shouldn't."

"Follow me," Wiggles said. "The smell is strongest in this direction."

I traipsed after Wiggles, pushing aside branches and trying not to stumble over too many hidden roots.

We were walking for about ten minutes, and the noises were growing louder.

Fallon burst through a bush, did a fancy somersault, and landed on her feet with a flourish. She thrust out her arms. "Have I got a surprise for you!"

"What are you up to, Fallon?" I said.

She jigged on her toes. "I've caught something incredible. You have to see it. He's huge, hairy, and he keeps growling."

My stomach plummeted to my boots. That sounded like Basil. "You'd better show us. He's not injured, I hope?"

"What if I have injured the beast? He was creeping around my woods. He deserves to be taught a lesson."

I gritted my teeth and shook my head as I followed Fallon through the trees with Wiggles, and we made our way into a small clearing.

Hanging over our heads was a sparkling green net. Basil was trapped inside.

"Look at that magnificent creature," Fallon said. "He walks on two legs, so he won't be any good for riding, but I can still put him to good use. He's enormous. He could help with the hard labor when I'm putting up my traps. No more climbing trees for me. Of course, I'll need to tame him."

"Fallon, that's Basil! He's not dangerous." I looked up at Basil. "Don't you understand the meaning of keeping a low profile?"

He groaned and scrubbed at his face. "I figured I could blend in with the shadows and no one would notice me."

"Nothing could hide you," Fallon said. "You're a giant. What kind of beast are you?"

"Basil's a Bigfoot," I said.

Fallon clapped a hand over her mouth and squeaked. She lowered her hand. "Even better. They're hardy creatures. Oh! And did you know they can slow time?"

"I did. Let him go. He's not yours to keep."

"He is. He's in my woods, so I claim ownership. Basil the Bigfoot, you belong to me."

Basil simply grumbled and curled into a ball. "I wish I'd never come to Willow Tree Falls."

"You'd better let him go," I said. "The angels are after him, and I need to make sure they don't find him."

"The angels can't have him. He's my work beast."

"They don't want him for free labor."

"What do they want him for?"

"Dazielle's got it into her head that Basil killed a woman. You must have noticed all the hunting parties in the woods."

Fallon grumbled several curse words under her breath. "I was tempted to slay the blundering idiots as they wandered around without a clue."

"I'm glad you resisted the urge," I said. "But Dazielle wants to question Basil about Sabine's murder."

"Is he involved?" Fallon's gaze turned suspicious. "I can always hide him, so long as he agrees to work for me. I'm sure we could come to a mutually beneficial arrangement. I can control a killer if I have to."

"Basil isn't a killer," I said.

"Most likely," Wiggles said. "We're sixty/forty in his favor as him being innocent."

Basil grunted. "I didn't do it."

"Okay, seventy/thirty," Wiggles said. "And I like you, whatever you've done."

"Forget the odds. Basil's still at risk of being arrested for something I'm pretty sure he didn't do," I said. "And he'll definitely be caught if you don't let him down."

"Please let me go," Basil said.

"Tempest came this way. I'm sure I saw her."

I tensed. That was Dazielle's voice. That devious angel, she'd followed me. She must have known I'd come after Basil to protect him.

Wiggles growled, and his eyes glowed. "We've got feathered trouble heading our way."

Fallon squeaked. She raced to a tree and started sawing through the netting holding Basil up.

"Hurry! We have to get him out of here," I said.

"I'm going as fast as I can," Fallon said. "This magic takes more than a few seconds to dissolve."

"Let me help." I thrust a blast of magic at the rope, and after several hits, it snapped.

Basil flew through the air. He bounced off the ground and rolled out of the netting and onto his feet.

"Let's move." I grabbed his arm.

"I can't go to prison," Basil said. "I'd never survive in a crowded jail."

"To make sure that doesn't happen, we have to move. Fallon, is there any chance you can run interference with the angels?"

"I could. But what's in it for me?"

"How about I don't march through the forest destroying all your traps?"

"Huh! That works. Leave it to me. They won't know what's hit them." She saluted me then dashed away through the trees.

I raced in the opposite direction with Basil and Wiggles. I had to get Basil away from the angels.

Large-winged shadows swooped over our heads, and I ducked, pulling Basil down with me.

"I'll distract them too," Wiggles said. He sucked in a breath and leaped away into the trees, crashing around to draw the angels' attention from us.

"I see you, Tempest. I'll arrest you if you're helping that criminal." Anger laced Dazielle's words as she swooped over our heads again.

I dodged into some thicker trees, yanking Basil along with me. I skidded to a halt, and Basil slammed into my back. An angel had just appeared in front of us.

"We need to go another way. If we head back to the swamp, get through that foliage and to your cave, it might be enough to shake off the angels."

There were several startled cries from over our heads and a yell of victory from Fallon. She was holding up her end of the bargain, but it wasn't enough. Two more angels appeared in front of us.

"We're trapped," Basil whispered. "Run. Save yourself."

"I'm not leaving you with the angels. They'll take you in."

"I can slow them down. My ability works on angels. I'll trap them here and then leave."

"Do it. Since these angels aren't listening to sense, we have to try something else."

Basil had just begun to spin his arm in a circle when a flash of red magic shot through the trees and slammed into an angel, knocking her off her feet.

I whipped my head around, trying to see who'd just blasted an angel.

"Is that a friend of yours?" Basil said, his arm still raised.

"No one else knows where I am," I said.

There was a second shot of the same powerful magic, and another angel shrieked and disappeared from view.

A tingle ran over my skin. I recognized that magic signature. I narrowed my eyes and squinted through the trees. "Zandra, is that you?"

Her head appeared from around the side of a tree, and she gave me a thumbs-up. "I'll deal with this lot. You make a run for it."

"Be careful. Don't hurt the angels."

She shook her head at me. "Of course I'll hurt them. They're messing with you and the furry guy. What have you done, anyway?"

"I can't explain now. Just take it easy on them."

She shooed me away then blasted more magic at an approaching angel. There was a sickening thud, and something snapped. I hoped it was a dry branch and not a wing or a bone.

I wanted to run, but I could sense Zandra's magic was unstable. She was hurting these angels and didn't seem to know how strong she was.

"Basil, that's my half-sister," I said. "She needs my help. She still learning how to use her powers."

His body shook as he nodded. "I feel her strength. Does she use dark magic?"

"I'm not sure what she uses, but it's not good. If she's not careful, she'll kill an angel, then we'll have more trouble on our hands." I dropped my hold on Basil. "You go to your cave. Don't stop. When it's quiet, I'll come find you."

"Be careful, Tempest." Basil cast a worried look at Zandra and then dodged away through the trees.

Zandra's laugh echoed through the woods as she blasted out more magic. With every spell she fired, the air sparked and heated.

I dodged around some trees and almost stepped on Jophiel. She was on the ground, one wing bent and a dazed look on her face.

I tried to help her to her feet, but she heaved out a breath and shook her head. "I've never been blasted with anything so strong before. Who's attacking us?"

"Don't worry about that. Stay where you are. I'll get help." I hurried away, edging nearer to Zandra.

"Zandra! Take a break. You're doing too much magic."

"The more I do, the stronger I get." She glanced over her shoulder. Her eyes were completely black. "Why are you still here?" She blasted another angel who shot over our heads, making her crash to the ground with a groan.

"Stop! You're hurting the angels."

"So? They want to hurt you. Isn't this what family is supposed to do, protect each other?"

My eyes widened as Zandra prepared a spell to fling at Dazielle, who had just appeared. I blasted out a knockback spell, slamming it into Zandra.

She staggered back but remained upright. "What are you doing? I'm trying to help."

"You're not in control of your magic."

Zandra powered up another spell.

I blasted her with a second knockback spell. Jeez, she was strong. She absorbed my magic as if it didn't affect her.

She hissed at me and slammed me with her own magic. Fortunately, it only skimmed my arm. Otherwise, I wouldn't be breathing.

I rubbed my aching arm as I scanned the trees for any sign of Basil. Good, he was gone. Hopefully, he'd have a big enough lead and escape the angels.

There was a scream and a loud thud.

I grimaced as another angel was downed. Just how powerful was Zandra? She was throwing out spells like they were free parade candy and didn't seem to be tiring.

As much as I hated to use him, Frank was lurking in the background, and I could sense him paying attention to Zandra, but he wasn't eager to make an appearance.

I lowered the barriers that kept him in check, and his energy slid up my spine in a sticky wave, heat curling through me as he unfurled.

I conjured another spell as I waited for Frank's energy to blast out. Nothing happened.

"Why are you holding back? You can take control any time you like. There's nothing stopping you," I said.

"I'm interested in the new addition to the village," he growled in my head.

"Focus on stopping her killing the angels."

"She has my full blessing. I'll just watch and see what happens."

I gritted my teeth and shoved the barriers back in place. Frank was no use to me, so I didn't want him around.

Three more angels descended through the trees, heading straight toward Zandra.

She backed away, jagged sparks of magic on her fingertips. Her eyes were glowing and her teeth bared. She looked barely human.

"We've got the creature!" someone yelled in the distance.

I turned around, my heart in my throat. They must mean Basil. I took a few steps in the direction the voice had come from but stopped and looked back at Zandra.

She threw another spell at the angels who were trying to trap her, firing out a dazzling shower of light, then turned and ran.

I looked at the carnage left behind. Several angels were wounded, two looked unconscious, and from the shouted protests in the distance, Basil had been captured.

This mission to escape was a disaster.

Chapter 15

I followed Dazielle and two other angels as they restrained Basil and led him back to Angel Force. "You've got the wrong person. He's not involved in this murder."

"And you're not involved in this case," Dazielle said. "Go home, Tempest. Your help isn't required."

"He's innocent," I said.

Basil's head hung low, and he shuffled his feet as he was dragged along. "They won't believe you. All they see is a monster. It's not my fault. I'm big and get hairy when I'm scared."

"You evaded capture," Dazielle said. "That makes you look guilty."

"You heard him. He's scared. He knows you'll think the worst."

"Take him inside Angel Force," Dazielle said to her angels. "I'll deal with this problem." She turned and glared at me.

"I'm not a problem. If you think Basil's the killer, you'll stop looking for anyone else. They'll get away with killing Sabine."

"I don't trust you. You knew that creature was hiding in the woods, and you hid him from us. This case could have been solved by now if you hadn't interfered."

"I was buying him time while I investigated. Basil wasn't going anywhere. I knew where he was."

"And who did you have helping you?" Dazielle said. "I've got three angels heading to the hospital because of your assistant. She's in trouble as well."

I also had a painful arm from where Zandra's magic had hit me. My half-sister was scarily powerful.

"She's a new witch in the village who didn't mean any harm. She thought I needed help. After all, your angels were chasing me."

"This witch needs to be stopped."

I didn't disagree, but I wasn't revealing any information about Zandra to Dazielle.

"Tempest, what's going on?" My dad hurried over as we emerged from the trees. "I heard there was a fight in the woods."

"Take your daughter away, Abel, before she finds herself in a cell." Dazielle didn't slow her pace as she marched past my dad.

"You want to arrest Tempest?" he said.

"Most days, I do. But this time, it's justified. Get her out of here," Dazielle tossed out over her shoulder.

Rage bubbled through me as I watched her go. Basil wasn't a killer, and Dazielle couldn't pin this murder on him, but she'd do her best to make him the perfect scapegoat.

Dad put an arm around my shoulders. "You look like you need a break. Come with me."

I shot one more glare at Dazielle. "Wait! Wiggles is still in the woods. We can't leave without him."

"I'm right here!" He emerged from the trees and shook out his fur. He was covered in mud and wagging his tail. "I just didn't want to be near Dazielle when she was being so mean to everyone."

I petted the one clean spot on his head. "Good work. We almost beat those angels. If there hadn't been so many of them, we'd have gotten Basil away safely."

"Let's go, and you can tell me what you're involved in." Dad walked beside me as we made our way into the village.

I sighed. "Dazielle's got this all wrong."

"I'm sure she does her best."

"Which isn't good enough if she's going to charge Basil with murder."

"Come back to the house. We'll talk about it over a coffee."

"And cake," Wiggles said. "Fighting angels makes me hungry."

"I'm sure I'll be able to find something for you to eat. Queenie brought over a tin of something this morning," Dad said.

We headed to the house, and Dad settled me at the table before switching on the kettle.

I took a few deep breaths as I got my thoughts in order. This felt like a mess. Basil had been arrested, Zandra was in trouble with the angels, and I didn't know who'd killed Sabine.

Uncle Kenny strolled into the kitchen. "Tempest! I got your note. Did you get to Basil in time to warn him?"

"No, the angels have him. We tried to stop them, but we weren't quick enough."

He sank into a chair. "Basil won't do well in a cell if they keep him for long."

Dad placed a tin of cookies on the kitchen table, along with three mugs of coffee, and then settled opposite me. "Tell us what happened."

I tossed Wiggles a cookie. "I was trying to stop the angels from arresting the Bigfoot. Has Uncle Kenny told you about him?"

Dad nodded. "He has. He sounds like an incredible creature."

"He is. And I don't think he's a killer." I sipped my coffee, welcoming the warmth as my muscles hummed with tension. "But the angels found out about him and assumed the worst, especially since he fit the description of the killer."

"I expect the angels believe everything written about Bigfoot. Most people believe Bigfoot are dangerous," Dad said.

"Which is scandalous nonsense," Uncle Kenny said.

I nodded. "I don't believe any of that. Basil was gentle when we met, and he just wants to be left alone. Anyway, I headed into the forest to warn him the angels were hunting him. By the time I got there, Fallon had accidentally trapped Basil. Then the angels arrived."

"Did an angel injure your arm?" Dad said. "You're holding it like you're hurt."

I let out another sigh. "No, that was Zandra."

"Zandra? She's been helping you hide Basil?"

"She wasn't helping. Dad, I'm worried about her. She's powerful and doesn't always have control of her magic. If the spell she'd thrown at me had been a direct hit, I wouldn't be breathing. Have you any idea how strong her abilities are?"

He took a long sip of his coffee before placing the mug down. "Not really. I'm not proud to admit I was a hands-off dad. I'm still in shock she used such a strong spell to grow up fast. Could that be what's causing her problems?"

"Maybe. But no one blames you for that. You had a lot going on. You weren't yourself. And you were a great dad to me and Aurora."

"I should have done more for Zandra. I left her mom to do the hard work and showed up to be the fun dad when required. It wasn't enough. I let her down. And this is the result."

"Zandra needs to find a way to channel her power. Her magic is off the charts strong. The spell she was using on the angels could have killed them."

"I'll talk to her, but my magic isn't a tenth of hers or yours. I'm not sure she'll believe me if I warn her to be careful."

"I've offered to help, and she wasn't against the idea, but we could need a stronger intervention. Zandra needs help from all the Crypt witches to get things under control. It never ends well when a witch loses her grip on her powers."

Dad grimaced. "Of course. We'll fix this. And I'm sure your mom will help."

"And we have another problem. Frank is interested in Zandra. I tried to draw on his power, but he wanted to see her in action. I don't want him going after another one of my sisters."

"Your demon's a threat to Zandra?"

"He's a threat to everyone. But he was interested in her. I need to keep them apart, but I also want to help her."

"Let me deal with Zandra for now. It's time to arrange that family get-together. She can see how the rest of you control your magic, and it might encourage her to do the same. Queenie and Dottie have years of experience in how to focus their magic, and I'm sure they'll want to make sure she's safe."

"We need to make her feel like she's part of this family. She's still living on the edges and isn't convinced we want her around."

Dad frowned. "That's on me as well. I'm trying to find a balance to make sure I don't upset Cora or Zandra."

"Mom is okay, though? It must be hard on her knowing Zandra is staying in the village."

"She's been great about it. But it's difficult. Zandra's here now, and she needs to be welcomed into the family."

"And I need to help her get control of her magic. If she'd killed an angel, that would have been it for her."

"Why was Zandra in the woods?" Uncle Kenny asked.

"I think she was trying to help me. Maybe she saw me go in there looking for Basil."

"I should speak to Dazielle," Uncle Kenny said. "Prove to her Basil isn't a threat. I can take her my research. That may convince her he didn't kill Sabine."

"It's worth a try, but that's another problem to deal with. Dazielle is way off her game, and she's making poor decisions."

"What do you mean?" Dad said.

"She thought Uncle Kenny killed Sabine, then Tate, and now she's convinced it's Basil. It's a big old mess, and I'm not sure how to solve it. Although..."

"You've got an idea?" Dad said.

"Nothing definite. But Sabine was stabbed. That's what killed her, but she had a bite mark on her neck, the same as the other women who were attacked. The bite marks also looked the same, so I'm assuming it's the same person doing the biting. And that person has a type. Our biter likes pretty women with long, dark hair. And something you said, Uncle Kenny, has been playing on my mind."

"What's that?"

"That Bigfoot and humans could have a relationship."

"Oh! It's anatomically possible. It's not something I'm aware of happening, though. It's uncommon."

"When the angels discovered the stab wound on Sabine, they thought two killers could be working together. What if it's not that? What if it's bad luck on Sabine's part?"

"Basil bit her because he's looking for a mate?" Dad said.

Uncle Kenny nodded. "They do that."

"Basil bit Sabine, but she ran off. Then her killer found her and stabbed her when she was weakened.

Whoever it was tried to hide the stab wound by inflicting it on her neck," I said.

"I'm still not sure why Basil is biting women. It's not exactly romantic," Dad asked.

"Basil has a red streak in his fur," I said. "He's entering mate mode. I read up on Bigfoot, and they're supposed to get red manes when they're mate seeking. Maybe Basil's streak is a sign he's looking for love."

"It's possible," Uncle Kenny said. "But seasonal mate markings are usually more pronounced, and the fur around a Bigfoot's neck completely changes to a rusty red and only on the males. I've never heard of a single stripe on a Bigfoot." He jumped up, left the room, and came back with a pile of papers. "It could be a variation on the design. Give me a minute to check my records."

I sipped my coffee and ate cookies as he raked through his research.

"If it is, that makes sense," I said. "From what I've read, Bigfoot have little control when they're in full-on mating mode."

"That's also true," Uncle Kenny said. "And they sometimes nibble their mates when they're looking for a match."

"Nibble?" I said. "You mean leave huge bite patterns on their flesh?"

He nodded. "If Basil was biting another Bigfoot, the marks wouldn't be prominent. And if he has been biting human women, he may not be completely aware of his actions. He'd be driven by a primal urge to seek a partner."

"He really does that by biting his mate?" Dad said.

"Bigfoot don't go in for dating or long romances. They discover a compatible mate by tasting her. The females are receptive to the bites because they want to find a mate too. The mingling of their... essences, for want of a better word, shows if they'll produce healthy offspring," Uncle Kenny said.

"Basil can't be mistaking human women for female Bigfoot," Dad said.

"Female Bigfoot are much smaller than the males," Uncle Kenny said. "And when Basil's lust is piqued, he won't be thinking clearly."

"And the women he targeted all had loads of long dark hair. From the back, they could look like a female Bigfoot," I said. "Basil grabbed them and took a bite before he realized what they were."

"So Basil bit Sabine, thinking she could be his love match? She escaped and ran into her killer?" Dad said. "But why was she killed?"

"I'm not certain, but I'm pretty sure Sabine used magic, and she was tangled up with Kirk Wrangler and his dubious magic exhibition."

"I'm hearing lots of complaints from residents about that place," Dad said.

"It's grim, but her involvement in that place could have gotten Sabine in trouble. Kirk is in the middle of this, I'm sure of it, but there's a problem."

"What's that?" Uncle Kenny said.

"He has a cast-iron alibi. He was with Tilly when Sabine was stabbed." I leaned back and pinched the bridge of my nose. "I must be missing something."

Dad squeezed my arm. "You'll figure this out. You always do. Your mom's been telling me about the cases you've worked on with the angels."

"Someone had to stop them from messing up, but they don't want my help anymore," I said. "I've been kicked off this case for helping Basil."

"You need to find a way to get back on the case, so you can see him," Uncle Kenny said. "All that noise and uncertainty will terrify him. He could say anything to get some quiet."

"Which means Dazielle could force a confession. And the mood she's in, I wouldn't put it past her to do just that."

Granny Dottie's black cat familiar trotted into the kitchen. She stopped beside me and swiped a paw at my leg.

"Are you hungry?" I glanced at her bowl. "There's plenty of food in there."

She swiped me again, this time with her claws out.

"Ouch! You don't need to do that."

The cat stood and walked to the door. She turned and looked at me, flicking her tail.

"She wants to show you something," Dad said. "It's probably rodent related. She's been leaving them on the doormat for people to step on."

"If it's a dead mouse, I'm not interested."

"She'll only scratch you again if you ignore her."

I looked at Wiggles, who was snoozing on the rug. So much for having a helpful hellhound to see off furry problems like this.

I stood and hurried after the cat, who was making her way to the front door. She scratched on it until I opened it and then ran outside.

The second I stepped onto the porch, I heard raised voices.

"They've got him!" a guy yelled.

"We'll make them bring him out," another guy shouted.

I jogged to the gate and looked along the lane. A crowd was marching toward the village.

"It's time that monster paid," a woman in the crowd shouted.

"Uh oh! This doesn't look good." I looked down at the cat. "Thanks for letting me know a mob is forming. They're after Basil."

She yawned and trotted away.

I raced back into the house. "Dad, Uncle Kenny, I've got to go. There's a mob descending on Angel Force. They want Basil."

"I'll come with you." Dad was already pushing back his seat.

"No, you stay here. The angels are already suspicious of Uncle Kenny's involvement, and I don't want you getting in trouble as well."

"I can handle a few angels," Dad said.

"I know you can, but you don't need to. I'll check things out and send Wiggles back if I need support. Come on, Wiggles. Let's move." We had to stop the crowd before they killed an innocent creature.

Chapter 16

I raced back to Angel Force with Wiggles by my side.

The crowd of angry monster hunters were outside the main door, fighting with three angels to get in. Dazielle was among them, and there was a spark of anger and fear in her eyes as she battled with a skinny redhead, who held a huge plank of wood.

"Get the beast out here so we can deal with it," someone yelled.

"You all need to calm down. We do have a suspect in custody for Sabine's murder, but he's not going anywhere," Dazielle said.

"It's a monster. It must be destroyed."

"We'll destroy it for you," someone else yelled. "Bring it out, or we're going in."

"Everyone go home," Dazielle said, "or you'll be arrested."

"You can't arrest all of us," someone shouted. "We're keeping this place safe. We demand to see the monster."

The crowd surged forward, and the angels were overwhelmed as fists and makeshift weapons struck them.

I shoved to the front of the crowd with Wiggles and yanked the redhead off Dazielle. "It looks like you could do with a hand."

She glared at me as she shoved another human away from the door. "I told you to stay away."

"I'm never good at following orders. You need me here. You can't use your powers on the humans. They'd think you're a monster, too."

Two people tripped over Wiggles as he placed himself strategically in their path.

Three more broke through the angels and headed for the door. They were stopped before they could get in, but it was only a matter of time before they smashed their way into the building. Then Basil's life would be at risk, and I wasn't letting that happen.

"What do you suggest we do?" Dazielle ducked as the redhead grabbed for her again.

Wiggles dodged through the crowd, barging into people and knocking them off balance. "Who knew human pinball could be such fun."

I looked around the crowd. There were at least thirty people. It would take most of my energy, but I could do it. "How about I convince them there's free food and a party at the stone circle?"

"You shouldn't use your magic on humans." Dazielle grabbed a guy's jacket and whirled him away from the door.

"It's a mass compulsion spell. It won't hurt them. It'll be diluted because there are so many of them, so there won't be any nasty side effects." I sidestepped a fuzzy-haired woman as she stumbled against me.

Dazielle was jumped on by two humans. She yelped and struggled to get them off her back. "Fine! Do it! But be careful. You know how fragile they are."

"Let us in!" a woman screamed in Dazielle's face. "We want to kill the beast."

I stepped to the edge of the crowd so I wouldn't be noticed sparking up a spell. All they needed was a little compulsion magic. I'd convince them there was an amazing free party and Basil wasn't here. It should get rid of most of them, and once the main crowd broke away, the rest would follow. The power of a mob mentality was sometimes useful to exploit, especially if it kept my friends safe.

I closed my eyes, took several deep breaths, and allowed the compulsion magic to pulse out of me in a slow moving wave. It hit those closest first then drifted through the rest of the crowd.

After a couple of minutes, the shouting faded. I opened my eyes and looked around. People mostly looked confused, and a few were already staggering away.

The angels were still tussling with several stubborn individuals. They must be the most eager to hurt Basil. I focused my magic on them.

It took several concentrated pulses of compulsion magic, and my brow was damp with sweat by the time they stopped fighting. They backed off and stared at the building.

"You don't need to be here." Dazielle smooth down her ruffled hair. "Go to the party like everyone else. There's nothing to worry about."

I kept my magic pulsing through the air until the stragglers left.

Dazielle let out a sigh. "What incited them to come here?"

"One guess," I said.

She scowled at me. "I'm not in the mood for guessing."

"Kirk! He wants Basil for his collection."

"If he incited this mob, where is he?"

I shrugged. "He could have been here and gotten lost in the crowd." A flash of something shiny beside a tree near the building made me peer into the gloom. "Or he could be keeping watch to see the damage he caused. Look over there." I pointed at the trees.

Dazielle didn't seem convinced. "What am I supposed to see?"

"Kirk the jerk. He's right over there, lurking in the shadows." And he wasn't alone. He had Oakley and Bella with him. Kirk looked furious as the crowd walked away. He was muttering something, and his hand was by his throat. Oakley and Bella looked bemused, as if they had no idea what they were doing.

But it was Kirk I was most interested in. The flash that had caught my eye looked like an amulet, and he was rubbing it. He must have been using a spell to manipulate the crowd.

"Do you know for certain Kirk instructed these people to attack Angel Force?" Dazielle said.

"No, but he's still my prime suspect, despite you thinking Basil killed Sabine. He's behind this. He got the crowd riled up by telling them you'd captured Basil. He sent them here."

"That's just a hunch. You have no proof."

"Maybe, but it's just the sort of sleazy thing he'd do."

"You don't like him. That's why you think he's involved."

"There's nothing to like, but he's behind this. And he could be using some kind of blocking spell because he hasn't been influenced by my magic."

"Neither have his friends. It's only because they're too far away."

"My magic would have reached them. Kirk's not affected because he's using magic himself. He has to be behind this."

"No, he's not. I've already ruled out Kirk," Dazielle said. "No one can be in two places at once. Unless you're doubting Tilly's word about his alibi."

"Of course not! Tilly is telling the truth. At least, she thinks she is. Maybe his magic affected her, too." I watched as Kirk, Oakley, and Bella disappeared into the gloom of the trees. Part of me wanted to go after them, but I also wanted to make sure Basil was okay. And now Dazielle was talking to me again, I had a way to get to him.

"Tilly is a powerful witch. It wouldn't be easy to influence her," Dazielle said.

"Kirk's gathered magic artifacts from all over the world. Who knows what power he's using. And I bet he has no idea how dangerous it is. Humans tinkering with things they don't understand leads to trouble."

"I'm still convinced Basil is behind this," Dazielle said. "He's barely spoken since we took him in. His silence is only making things look worse for him."

I turned to face her, trying not to back away at the anger glinting in her eyes. "I know you think it was wrong that I kept him a secret, but I did it because I knew you'd see him as a monster."

"I don't see him as a monster. I see him as a criminal."

"Let me talk to Basil."

"No, you're off this case."

"I might be able to get him to open up."

"Or you'll convince him to keep quiet, so I'll never get a confession."

I lifted my hands. "If Basil is guilty, then I'll support you. And..." How much should I reveal about a Bigfoot's mating urges and the possibility he had bitten those women?

"And..." she tapped her foot.

"I don't think Basil is completely innocent. But he's not a killer."

She was silent for a long time, staring into the growing gloom. "You won't leave this alone until I let you in, will you?"

"Not until justice is done. And if you charge Basil with a crime he didn't commit, I'll keep hassling you."

Dazielle scowled at me. "Then you'd better come this way."

I silently cheered as we headed into Angel Force and into the main office. The angels working in there looked glum, which was unusual.

"Is something going on?" I asked.

"It's nothing you need to worry about," Dazielle said.

I narrowed my eyes as I looked around again. "Where's Dominic?"

She pursed her lips. "He no longer works here."

I turned and stared at her. "You fired him over that blog?"

"What was I supposed to do? I've put up with so much nonsense from that angel. This was the final straw."

"But it's Dominic. He never means to do anything wrong. He's made a few mistakes in the past, but you can't sack him."

"He posted information about magic for anyone to read. He thought it was fun and didn't see the consequences of his dangerous actions."

I lifted one shoulder. "It wasn't his smartest move, but it wasn't malicious."

"It was the dumbest move he's ever made. I can't overlook this. I can handle him messing up the files or forgetting to record witness names. I can even forgive him when he muddles his shifts and doesn't turn up when he's supposed to but not this. He was feeding information to Kirk, which led him to us. Dominic put the sanctity of Willow Tree Falls at risk. All because he got nice comments about what he was posting."

"Dominic just wants to be friends with everyone. He always sees the good in people and never realizes they might use him."

"Then he can't work for Angel Force. He's supposed to uphold the law, and he almost destroyed this place by his inability to keep quiet."

"What will he do now?"

"That's not my problem. He was a liability, and he's gone."

I wasn't done fighting Dominic's corner. Yes, it was a foolish move to post that information, and yes, it meant we had Kirk hanging around and causing problems, but Dominic was one of the innocents. He still believed everyone was basically decent. He shouldn't be punished for that.

But I needed to concentrate on Basil first. Save the Bigfoot then save the angel.

"Where's Basil?" I said.

"In a cell. We didn't want to risk him breaking out if we left him in an interview room."

"He shouldn't be behind bars. Get him out and we'll speak to him. I'll prove to you he didn't kill Sabine."

Dazielle gestured at a glum-faced angel as she headed to the cells. "Come with me. We'll release the prisoner."

Wiggles trotted to the refreshment table and sniffed around. "You can definitely tell Dominic's not here. There are no cookies. He always brought good cookies into work."

I joined him and made myself another coffee. I had a feeling it would be a long night, and I needed to be heavily caffeinated. "Dominic can't lose his job. What else will he do if he's not working here?"

"You could offer him a job at Cloven Hoof."

"That wouldn't work. A former Angel Force employee would scare away the customers. They'd think he was watching to see if they did anything wrong. I'll get him his job back. It's not fair he's being punished because Kirk's a tricky weasel."

"Basil is ready for us," Dazielle said from the other side of the room. "This way."

I entered the interview room behind Dazielle. Basil was slumped in a seat that was too small for him, his head down and his arms resting on the table in front of him.

"Hey, Basil. Try not to worry. I'll get you out of here as soon as possible." I settled in the seat opposite him, and Dazielle took the seat next to me.

"Don't make promises you can't keep," she muttered.

Basil sighed. "I tried to do the right thing."

Dazielle glanced at me. "You're confessing to Sabine's murder?"

"Oh! No! I didn't kill her." His panicked gaze shot to me.

"Did you do anything to her?" I asked as gently as possible. Basil was already shaking from head to toe and needed to be handled carefully.

His expression was full of shame as he glanced at me. "There are times when I'm not always in control of myself."

"Does this have something to do with you looking for a mate?"

He lowered his head. "Yes."

"What are you talking about?" Dazielle said, her tone sharp.

Basil shuffled his butt in his seat. "I... I bit Sabine."

"I knew it! And she wasn't the first woman you attacked." Dazielle whacked a hand on the table. "Was Sabine the first to fight back, so you had to silence her?"

"Let Basil speak," I said. "He has a reason for biting."

"I... I do. I'm looking for love." Basil stroked a hand over the red stripe in his hair. "When Bigfoot seek mates, our instincts take over."

"You had no option but to bite these women?" Dazielle's nostrils flared. "You'll have to do better than that."

"He's telling the truth. When a male Bigfoot is ready to find a mate, his fur changes color. The red stripe on Basil's head isn't common, but it's a sign his lust is up."

Basil's cheeks glowed. "I do feel amorous. And my stripe is unusual. Not many female Bigfoot like it, so I've had a lot of rejection. Most males develop a stunning scarlet ruff around their neck, but my color change only appears in my hair. It fades when I no longer seek a female."

"It's like the werewolf instinct when there's a full moon," I said to Dazielle. "Basil's only focus is to find a mate."

Her narrowed eyes suggested she didn't believe either of us. "If that's the case, why are you biting humans? How does that have anything to do with finding a mate?"

"You never studied Bigfoot 101?" I said.

She glared at me. "I'm waiting for an answer."

Basil sighed again. "I'm not as big or hairy as some Bigfoot. I was the litter runt. A late bloomer."

"You're my first Bigfoot," I said. "You look big to me."

He smiled. "Thank you, but I'm not. I'm considered feeble. It's why I don't have much success with females. And there's a rumor that, many generations back, a female Bigfoot and a human male mated and produced offspring. I'm from that family line. I may be part-human and part-Bigfoot. It means I'm compatible with humans. They're not my first choice, but my options are limited."

"I'm not interested in your family history. I want to know why you bit those women," Dazielle snapped.

"They weren't attack style bites; they were love bites," I said. "Well, testing for love bites. Bites to see if they were compatible."

"It's more of a love nip," Basil said. "Female Bigfoot expect it from males. It's a way to see if we're suitable to be together."

"Those women you attacked were terrified. They thought they were going to die, and Sabine did," Dazielle said.

"I am sorry about that. I wasn't thinking straight. My lust was up when I saw all that striking dark hair. Something in me triggered, and I had to see if they were right for me. I feel terrible for upsetting them."

"So you admit to attacking them?" Dazielle said.

Basil's gaze dipped. "I do. It's not something I'm proud of, but I only took a small bite. I barely drew blood."

"You drew more than a little blood from Sabine," Dazielle said. "Admit you killed her, and we can close this case."

"No! I didn't. I promise you. I'll confess to harming the other humans and biting Sabine, but it wasn't until I'd sunk my teeth into their necks that I came to my senses and realized what I was doing. I stopped immediately and ran off. By then, it was too late."

"What happened when you bit Sabine?" I said.

"It was awful. She screamed so loudly it hurt my ears, so I let her go. And she wasn't the one for me. She tasted strange and had an herby flavor to her blood. It wasn't pleasant."

I sat forward in my seat. "An herby flavor? What would Sabine be using to make her blood taste strange? Was she sick and using a herbal remedy or a spell to treat herself?"

Dazielle shook her head. "The autopsy showed she was healthy. And nothing unusual showed on her blood work."

"Which means magic could be involved. Someone was using magic on Sabine. That's why her blood tasted funky."

"I've never tasted anything like it," Basil said. "I don't like to disrespect the dead, but it was gross."

I turned to Dazielle. "This makes sense. Whoever killed Sabine must have witnessed Basil bite her. They—"

"If you don't mind, I prefer the phrase love nip," Basil said. "Female Bigfoot enjoy the experience."

"Basil, I'm happy to help get you off this murder charge, but you bit several women without their consent. That's a crime." Basil may have been in the mating mood, but that didn't justify him biting whoever he liked.

His head lowered again. "I really didn't mean any harm."

I kept my focus on Dazielle. "The killer saw Basil bite Sabine and couldn't miss the opportunity to get her when she was vulnerable. Basil's bite mark was used to conceal the fatal wound. Maybe whoever did this hoped Basil would take the fall, and the stab wound would be missed."

"A stab wound doesn't tie in with your magic assumption," Dazielle said.

"They used a knife to throw us off the magic scent," I said.

"Or Basil used a knife to make us think he wasn't involved," Dazielle said.

"He wouldn't need a knife to kill Sabine," I said. "Basil could have easily ripped off her head with his bare hands."

He grimaced but nodded. "I'd never do that, but I could. And I don't like knives. I'll confess to biting the women, but when I left Sabine, she was alive."

Dazielle heaved out a sigh. "Even if you didn't kill Sabine, you're in serious trouble. Biting without permission is a crime."

At last, we were getting somewhere if Dazielle was considering Basil innocent of murder. I felt sorry for him, but he'd messed up. He couldn't get away with those love nips, but I hoped the judge would be lenient on him.

"So, if not Basil, are you going to go after Tate again?" I said to Dazielle.

Her eyes narrowed. "It's possible."

"Or Uncle Kenny?"

Her glare shifted to me. "He was found with the victim's blood on him."

"Or how about we focus on someone who's much more likely to have wanted Sabine dead?" I said.

"Who do you have in mind?"

I arched my eyebrows. I knew a sneaky, smug individual who'd enjoy hurting Sabine. "It's time to talk to Kirk again. He's tangled up in this murder, and I just need to figure out how he did it."

Chapter 17

It took Dazielle an hour to go through everything with Basil. She'd taken his statement, and he was being returned to a cell as I left Angel Force with Wiggles to hunt out Kirk and get the truth out of him.

I hurried over to Tilly's restaurant to see if she could give me any more information about Kirk's alibi. All I needed was a chink in his armor, and I'd get him.

It was the late dinner rush, so there weren't many spare tables, but I squeezed into a small corner seat and waved at Tilly.

She grinned back at me and nodded. "I'll be two minutes."

I settled in, surrounded by the buzz of people enjoying their food, but I barely noticed the tempting scents drifting from the kitchen. Kirk was manipulating everyone, and I was sure he'd found a way to use magic. Could he have set this whole thing up? He'd come to Willow Tree Falls knowing Basil was looking for a mate and planned to use him as a scapegoat. Kirk could have made sure Sabine was in the woods with the hunting parties at the same time as Basil. Basil definitely had a type, and Sabine fit the profile.

Kirk could have done his research on Bigfoot, tracked Basil to the village, and set his plan in motion. Maybe he even hoped Basil would kill Sabine, but when he only injured her, Kirk had to finish the job.

Tilly arrived by the table. "From your expression, I imagine you're in the mood for cake." She set down a large slice of chocolate fudge cake.

My eyes widened, and I licked my lips. I'd barely noticed my hunger until I was presented with that feast. "Thanks, I could do with a boost, but I'm actually here to double-check Kirk's alibi."

"You still think he's involved in Sabine's murder?" Tilly glanced around at her busy tables to make sure no one needed her.

"He's got devious liar written all over him." I took a bite of the cake and let out a contented sigh. Cake always made things feel better.

"I wish I had better news for you, but I gave it some serious thought after we last spoke. Kirk was here that night. He enjoyed his meal, had several drinks, and even chatted to other people."

"He didn't slip out at any time?"

"Only for a couple of minutes, when he went to the washroom. Kirk wouldn't have had time to get to the woods and deal with Sabine."

"What if he used magic?"

Tilly shook her head. "Kirk isn't a magic user. He couldn't do a transportation spell."

"I'm not thinking about transportation magic. What if he used magic on you and the other customers to convince you he was here, when he'd really snuck out to stab Sabine?"

She snorted a laugh. "Do you really think a non-magic user with some off-the-shelf spell would have any effect on me?"

I grinned at her. Tilly was a powerful witch, and it would take more than your standard spell to bother her.

"It's an idea," I said. "Kirk could have used something to make you think he was here all the time."

"He wouldn't have dared. And if he had, he'd never do it again. Trust me, he didn't use magic on me."

"What about magic artifacts? If you believe one tenth of what he tells people, that exhibition he hauls around the country is full of magical items. He could have brought something in with him and that affected you."

Tilly's mouth twisted to the side. "If he did, then he concealed it well. I didn't feel any strange magic while he was here. And something that powerful would have given off a vibe."

"What about an amulet? Was Kirk wearing any jewelry?"

"Actually, he was. He had it around his neck. I figured it was a tourist trinket. You can get things like that in several of the stores in the village."

"Did you sense anything unusual about the amulet?"

"No, nothing." Tilly turned as someone called for her. "I'll be with you in a minute."

"Kirk has to be using something that allows him to move around the village and do what he likes while giving himself an alibi. It has to be something powerful he's carrying on his person."

"I wish I could be of more help, but I've got to go," Tilly said. "People are getting hungry, and hungry people make for grumpy customers and poor tippers."

"Sure. Thanks. I just needed to see if I could find a flaw in Kirk's alibi."

"No problem. If I think of anything else, I'll let you know. Enjoy your cake." Tilly hurried away.

I ate a couple more bites of the rich chocolate fudge cake. I needed to see the amulet Kirk wore. If I could get my hands on it, I could reveal the magic it contained.

I'd just finished my last bite of cake and was ready to confront Kirk when Mom hurried past the restaurant.

My heart sped up at the stern expression on her face. She was usually smiling, but I had a good idea what was making her look so serious.

I paid for my cake then paused as I stepped outside. I needed to get the truth out of Kirk as soon as possible, but my family needed me. Mom could be having a tough time with Zandra being here.

"Good cake?" Wiggles head-butted my leg.

"Yes. Tilly always makes excellent cake." I turned to look up the hill at the stone circle and then at my mom as she continued along the street.

"Where's my slice?" Wiggles said.

"Um... I forgot." Mom or Kirk? Who to tackle first?

Smoke billowed out of Wiggles' mouth. "How could you forget that I needed cake?"

"I promise I'll make it up to you. Come on."

"Come on! But... but cake!"

"Wiggles. Mom needs me. You'll get your cake another time." Decision made. It was always family first. "Mom, wait up!"

Wiggles grumbled under his breath as he stomped behind me.

My mom turned and smiled, but she looked distracted as she bent and petted Wiggles. "Tempest! Sorry, I didn't see you."

"No problem. I was in Tilly's when I saw you go past. Is everything okay?" I fell into step with her.

"Yes, everything's fine. I'm just busy."

"Have you spoken to Dad recently?"

"Of course. We saw each other this morning."

"I mean, have you talked about anything in particular?" Dad had said he was going to sort things out, but I didn't know how far he'd gotten with Zandra.

"Everything is good." She dug around inside her purse. "Oh, I must have left my wallet behind. I keep doing that, forgetting things. It must be my age."

I put a hand on her arm. "Or it could be that you're stressed."

She lifted her head. "What have I got to be stressed about?"

I raised my eyebrows but didn't say anything.

Mom sighed. "You've been talking to your dad about Zandra?"

"Yes, a bit. It must be so strange for you, having her around."

"It's something I'm getting used to, but it's nothing you need to worry about."

"I do worry. She's my half-sister, but you're my mom."

"You're right. Zandra is your sister. I'm trying to accept that, but..."

"I get it. Dad had this whole other life. It's going to be weird. You're allowed to freak out about it. I would."

She squeezed my hand. "I'm not freaking out, and I want to do the right thing. It's not Zandra's fault or your dad's that things got strange when he disappeared. It's not an ideal situation, but Zandra is family. And I heard she's all grown up. No longer a child. That must be hard for her. She... she needs me."

"She'll be glad to know that. I think she could do with help with her magic," I said.

Mom's eyes instantly filled with concern. "Is it the age spell? What's she struggling with?"

"Zandra's strong. I mean, you, Granny Dottie, and Auntie Queenie combined strong, but she doesn't have control when she does spells. Things get out of control. I'm worried she could hurt someone."

"Do you know about her magic origins?"

"Nope. Only what she got from Dad."

"No other magic user can do what we do. Our abilities are unique. We have the natural witch power, but we have the connection to the cemetery and the power to take down demons. Not many witches can do that. Do you think Zandra's not directing her power in the right place?"

"I do. And she'd probably like to know how to burn off some of that energy. It would help with her focus and control." And hopefully help me when she worked at Cloven Hoof. I didn't want to find the place burned to the ground because Zandra's magic went loco.

"Yes, I'm sure that's true." Mom tugged at her purse strap. "I should do more. I'm trying. I should get to know her."

"Is there anything stopping you, other than the obvious?"

Mom was quiet as she chewed on her bottom lip. I rarely saw her uncertain of anything, so I could tell this was a big deal. "I don't know how I'll feel when I meet her. Your dad said she looks a lot like you."

"She does. She behaves like me as well. Well, when I was a grumpy teenager with an attitude and thought I knew it all."

"You still have an attitude." Mom kissed my cheek. "But it's time I face this. Avoiding it doesn't mean it's not an issue."

"We'll face it together. And Zandra could be a good fit to help at the cemetery. I've given her some shifts at the club, but she's not a natural people person. It's caused a few issues. I imagine, with her abilities, she'd be great at demon whacking."

"It's good of you to help her. And it's a possibility. Your grandma's not getting any younger. I worry she takes too many shifts at the demon prison."

"She loves it there. And don't let Grandma Dottie hear you say she's too old to keep those demons in line."

Mom smiled. "I wouldn't dare. Now, I'd better go find my wallet, or I'll worry I've lost it."

As Mom walked away, I hoped I could help her figure this out. Having Zandra around was strange, and I wouldn't want to be in her position, not sure where I fit in the family or even if I was wanted. I'd felt that more than a few times when I'd been struggling to control Frank. My family loved me, but sometimes, it would have been easier for them if I wasn't around, messing things up with my badly behaving demon.

"Please tell me we're going to get some cake for me now," Wiggles said.

"We need to hunt down Kirk," I said. "He's behind what happened to Sabine. He's using magic to get away with murder, and I'm not letting that happen."

Wiggles dropped to his belly. "Then you need to carry me. I'm too weak to move. I need an immediate cake injection."

"Get off your furry belly and help me track a killer."

He rolled on his back and kicked his stubby legs. "Cake!"

"Killer!"

"Feed me cake."

I groaned. He could be a brat when he didn't get his own way.

Wiggles flipped over. "Hey, there's Oakley and Bella. Maybe they know where I can find a new owner who'll feed me cake on demand."

"In your furry dreams. But let's see how they're doing, and they may know where I can find Kirk and wring the truth out of him."

Chapter 18

"Hi, Tempest." Bella's smile was pensive as I walked up to them.

"Hey. I'm glad I ran into you," I said.

"We were just looking for somewhere to eat," Oakley said.

"Have you heard the latest about Sabine?"

Bella bit her lip. "Oakley told me about your conversation with him, and we saw the fight at the station. They have someone in custody?"

I nodded. "Why were you watching the fight?"

"We weren't. I mean, we were, but we were walking past when we heard shouting and came to take a look," Oakley said.

"You're friends with Kirk now? He was there, too."

"No way! But we bumped into him and couldn't shake him off," Oakley said. "He's into Bella."

"Gross! No, he's not." Bella's expression was anxious as she looked at me. "Do you really think Sabine was killed?"

"Sorry, I do. It's been confirmed following the autopsy. The bite on her neck wasn't fatal. She was stabbed."

"Oh!" Bella's face paled. "Who would want Sabine dead?"

"Actually, I wanted to talk to you about Kirk Wrangler," I said.

Oakley scowled. "You mentioned him when we talked at the museum. Did he have something to do with what happened to Sabine?"

"I'm looking into him, along with some other suspects," I said. "What do you know about Kirk?"

"I don't like the guy," Oakley said.

Bella glanced up at him. "You like everyone."

"Nope. Not Kirk."

"How do you know Kirk?" I said to him.

"I met him a couple of times," Oakley said.

"When was this?"

Oakley stuffed his hands into his jeans pockets. "When I met Sabine just after she took the job with him."

"I didn't know that," Bella said.

He scuffed his foot along the ground. "I didn't want to get your hopes up. I wanted Sabine back and thought, if we met and talked things through, I could convince her we could make a go of it. I'm glad I didn't tell you, because it didn't work out great. Sabine was busy both times, and Kirk kept hanging around, like he didn't want me there. He's a creepy dude."

"I'm so sorry it didn't work out," Bella said. "I loved you two as a couple."

Oakley cleared his throat and looked away. "Yeah, so did I."

"What made you think Kirk was creepy?" I said.

"I think he was into Sabine. He kept touching her arm and making inappropriate comments." Oakley looked at Bella. "You know what Sabine was like. She kept her head down and got on with things. She didn't want any trouble."

"Sabine was a born people pleaser," Bella said. "And she hated letting anyone down. She never liked to offend anyone, even if they were horrible. And from what she said, Kirk was an awful boss."

"Sabine kept making excuses for Kirk when I asked her about him. She even convinced me to have a drink with him one evening to show me he wasn't so bad. Well, I had one, but Kirk had way too much. And he freaked me out because he kept talking about magic like it was real."

I arched an eyebrow. "After visiting our wonderful museum, you still don't believe in magic?"

Oakley huffed out a quiet laugh. "I don't know what to believe. But Kirk isn't to be trusted."

"I'm not a fan either," Bella said. "Sabine spoke about him, and you're right about the magic thing. She was always saying Kirk was on the hunt for artifacts that were supposed to contain magic. Sabine used to get so excited about it. I could never figure out if she was joking, but she'd spend hours researching the artifacts for the exhibition."

"It sounds like Sabine believed in magic," I said.

"She most likely did, but I don't understand how magic can be real," Bella said. "But it made Sabine happy, so I didn't mind. It was her quirk."

This information only made me more convinced that Kirk was behind her murder. He knew magic was real, and perhaps Sabine had stumbled across information he'd let slip. He realized what he'd done and needed to silence her. Or Sabine may have wanted in on the magic, and he'd resented that. It was a good motive for wanting her dead.

My gaze dropped to the black band around Bella's neck. "Are you wearing a necklace?"

"Oh, yes." Bella pulled it out. It was a small teardrop shaped piece of amber, set in a leather binding.

"Where did you get that?" I said.

"Kirk gave it to me. We both got one," Bella said. "He said they were a gift since we were friends of Sabine."

"He was smarming up to us because he fancied Bella," Oakley said.

She thumped his arm. "Yuck! I'd never want anything to do with him."

"He kept asking if you wanted to see his special collection." Oakley waggled his eyebrows.

"Did you both get amulets?" I asked.

Oakley nodded. "Sure."

"Let's have a look at yours," I said.

He lifted it from under his shirt. "I'm not much into jewelry, but I guess this is okay, not too feminine. And Sabine liked it on me."

"Kirk sells them at the exhibition," Bella said. "Mine's pretty. I like it."

So Kirk was handing out amulets to Sabine's friends. He could be using the stones to control them and make sure they didn't dig into her murder too much.

"May I take a closer look?" I held the amulet Bella had around her neck, trying to sense magic in it.

There was something, but it wouldn't reveal itself. The magic was buried deep inside the stone.

"Um, is everything okay, Tempest?" Bella stepped back and tugged the amulet out of my grip. "You look kind of intense. I'm sure Kirk can sell you an amulet if you like this one."

"Oh, sure. Thanks." I tore my focus from the amulets. "Just be careful around Kirk. He's under investigation."

Her eyes widened a fraction. "Do you think he's a danger to us? I just figured he was a creepoid."

"No, but stick together and you'll be fine." This mystery led back to Kirk. He was using magic to manipulate people, and I had to get him off the streets before he messed with anyone else. I had no clue how many people he was affecting with his magic, or what the long-term effects would be.

"That's what we plan to do," Bella said.

"Sure," Oakley said.

"Do you have any idea where Kirk is?" I asked.

"I saw him go in the Ancient Imp not so long ago. He could still be there," Oakley said.

"Thanks." I was already turning toward the pub.

"We can help if you like," Oakley said. "I want to know if he did something to Sabine."

"I'll keep you informed if we get any new developments. Just stay safe. This will be over soon." I raced off with Wiggles to the Ancient Imp.

It was busy inside as I pushed through the crowd and looked around for Kirk. He was easy to spot. He stood in the center of the bar, waving his arms around, while a small crowd of tourists looked on.

"I'm going behind the bar to hunt out food before I faint." Wiggles grumbled at me as he mooched away.

"Stay out of trouble and don't bother Petra," I muttered, my attention on Kirk.

"I was seconds from death." Kirk looked around the group as several people gasped. "That's right. My life was flashing before my eyes. This enormous, evil creature with glowing red eyes stalked toward me. Saliva dripped from its jagged fangs, and its growl was so loud and deep it made the ground rumble."

There were several nervous chuckles from the enraptured audience.

"What lies are you making up now?" I muttered as I inched closer to Kirk.

"How did you kill the beast?" someone from the crowd said.

Kirk took a long sip of his drink. "Over my many years working with magic artifacts, I've managed to unleash some of their powers. I've only been able to tap into a fraction of what they can do, but my exhibition is full of these incredible discoveries. There are stones that enhance your strength and powders that render you invisible."

"I can think of plenty of fun uses for something like that," a guy called out.

Several people laughed.

Kirk ignored him. "I harnessed the power of an enchanted gem as the beast attacked. He tried to bite my throat, but I punched him in the chest and sent him flying. I thought the monster would run away, but it came for me again. It grabbed me in its huge paws, and we grappled to the ground. Its foul breath was in my face as it tried to bite me. So... I did the only thing I could."

"What did you do?" a wide-eyed woman at the front said.

"I thrust my hand into its mouth. I was holding the enchanted gem, and I threw it down the monster's throat. The creature convulsed several times and then vanished."

"It ran off?" the woman asked.

"No, it literally vanished into thin air." Kirk spread his fingers and made a poofing sound.

No one said anything for several seconds.

"And that was how I defeated the evil creature and rid the world of one more dangerous, bloodthirsty beast." Kirk gave a nod. "Just like the one I helped to trap after it killed my wonderful assistant."

I slid over to the bar as he launched into another tall tale and gestured to Petra Duke, owner of the Ancient Imp. "How long has this been going on?"

She rolled her eyes and pushed her black hair off her face. "Too long. Although he's bringing in the crowds, so I'm busy and the money's rolling in. I shouldn't complain, but the guy won't shut up."

"How many evil creatures as he claimed to have killed?"

"That's his third," she said.

"And it'll be his last."

Petra's eyes widened, and a smile slid across her face. "Has he done something wrong?"

"He has. I just need to prove it." I pushed through the crowd and headed over to Kirk. "That's enough monster hunting nonsense for one day."

Kirk glared at me. "What are you talking about? There's plenty more to share, and I haven't sold tickets for my exhibition yet."

I stepped closer and lowered my voice. "I doubt you'll want an audience when you tell me how you used magic to murder Sabine."

The color drained from Kirk's face as he glared at me. He looked around. "Did you just accuse me of being a murderer?"

I glanced at the watching crowd. If he wanted people to hear, it was fine by me. "What did Sabine do to make you so angry you killed her?"

"Be careful, Tempest. I have plenty of witnesses here who'll back me up about that night. I was nowhere near Sabine."

I raised my voice. "Yet you're still a suspect in a murder case."

Several people gasped, and murmuring began behind us.

Anger glinted in Kirk's eyes. "I'm innocent. Sabine was a good worker, and I respected her. Her death was a tragedy. One that can be avenged because the beast who savaged her is in captivity, thanks to me."

"That beast didn't kill her. Sabine was stabbed."

More breathy gasps came from the watching crowd. They'd have a tale to tell their families when they got home.

"Do you really want to do this with an audience?" I said to Kirk. "It could affect ticket sales."

Sweat beaded on Kirk's forehead. "I have nothing to hide."

"Then you won't mind revealing to everyone that you're not what you seem. Why don't you show these people the magic you claim to be able to use? Or how about using an enchanted gem and showing off its power?"

He choked out a laugh. "I can't conjure magic. Supernatural abilities are only available to the weird and wonderful creatures I pursue or in the artifacts I find. I simply help to open people's minds to how incredible the world is."

"You must have picked up a few tricks," I said. "Show us what you can do. Or are you scared your adoring crowd will turn against you? Does using magic make you a monster, too?"

"This woman is drunk," a guy behind me said. "Get her out of here. We want more monster stories, not magic hokum."

I turned and glared at him. "You believe in werewolves enough to race around our woods trying to kill them. Why not magic spells?"

The guy glowered at me, his stubbled face turning red as he took a sip of his beer.

I looked back at Kirk. The smugness radiating off him made me want to shoot a spell in his face, but we had an audience, and they were paying attention.

I glanced down at his neck, not surprised to see his amulet in place. That was how he was controlling things.

"Sabine figured out you were manipulating people," I said. "She wanted to put a stop to it."

"I don't manipulate people. I welcome them to my exhibitions. I open their eyes to—"

"I don't mean the magic trinkets you pedal. I'm talking about that." I jabbed a finger at the amulet. "Where did you get it?"

His hand went to the amulet, and he looked at it, a flicker of confusion crossing his face. "Why is that important?"

"She's crazy," the same guy muttered.

I ignored the insult. "Confess to killing Sabine. You're not leaving Willow Tree Falls until you do."

"Again, I'd advise you to be careful, Tempest. It's not sensible to threaten people. I can leave any time I choose, and there's nothing you can do to keep me here." Kirk leaned so close I could smell his cologne. "The first time we met, I knew there was something different about you. Perhaps you'll be the next magical creature I hunt."

Wiggles appeared by my side and growled at the same time as me. A hot wave of Frank's energy slid up my spine as he responded to the threat from Kirk.

Kirk recoiled as he stared at me. He must have seen my demon peeking out. Frank could be a nightmare, but sometimes you needed a nightmare to deal with creeps.

The muttering in the crowd stopped as everyone appeared to sense a change in the atmosphere.

"I could kill him, but humans are never a challenge," Frank muttered inside my head. "Although I may make an exception. He's a cocky one."

It was tempting to let Frank loose on Kirk and beat the truth out of him. I took a few deep breaths, taking a moment to get Frank under control.

Kirk adjusted his shirt collar and cleared his throat several times. "You need to leave. Everyone heard you making threats toward me. Get out of here before..."

"Before what?"

"I'll have you arrested." Kirk stepped back and bumped up against the wall.

"I'm going nowhere until you've told me the truth." My voice was only slightly growly from where Frank had tried to take control.

Kirk edged around me. "Then I'll leave. And you won't be able to stop me."

"What about the monster being held by the police?" someone in the crowd said. "It has to die."

"Yes, Kirk. What about the beast? You have to prove to everyone what an amazing monster hunter you are. Imagine the ticket sales when word gets out," I said.

Kirk slid a glance my way then pulled himself upright. "I'll speak to the police and make sure the creature is destroyed."

Several people groaned.

"We were promised a monster hunt," a woman said. "Maybe there are more monsters in the woods. We could go out again tonight."

"No one is hunting in our woods," I said. "They're out of bounds."

"No, they're not." The guy who'd been dumb enough to call me crazy gave me a hard nudge. "We're going hunting, and you can't stop us."

The confidence from the crowd seemed to buoy Kirk, and smugness slid back onto his face.

I reached forward and yanked the amulet off his neck. Its power fizzled on my skin. I couldn't detect the spell in it, but it was dark and intense as it trickled up my arm. I shoved it into my pocket just as Kirk groaned and collapsed to the floor.

There was a second of silence then the crowd exploded into action.

People swarmed around Kirk, trying to get him to wake up.

I backed away with Wiggles. I hadn't expected Kirk to react like that when I took the amulet.

"We need to get out of here," Wiggles muttered.

"Good idea." I turned and walked into someone's hard chest. I stepped back to see the guy who'd insulted me standing in my way.

"You're going nowhere." He grabbed me by the shoulders. "I saw what you did."

I shoved him and tried to step around him, but he blocked my path. "You don't want to do this." Frank was simmering just beneath the surface and itching for a fight.

"Don't let her go. She killed Kirk!" A shrill woman raced over and glared at me, and several more people joined her.

"He's not dead, is he?" I shot a worried look at Kirk, who still lay on the floor.

"What did you do to him?" the shrill woman said. "One second he was standing in front of you, and the next—"

"She hit him. I saw it," the guy next to her said. "She punched him."

"I didn't hit him. I simply..." How could I explain I yanked a magic amulet off his neck and he passed out? That would make me look insane and add fuel to the fire of this already angry crowd.

"Then she poisoned him!" the shrill woman said.

"I barely touched him. Maybe he fainted. It's hot in here. Or he could have had too much to drink."

"He was fine until you arrived and threatened him." The guy I'd walked into made another grab for me.

More people surrounded me and Wiggles. I wasn't getting out of this unless I was prepared to hurt some humans.

Petra dashed out from behind the bar and waded into the crowd. "Everyone calm down. I've called the authorities."

"This woman injured Kirk," the shrill voiced woman said. "We can't wait for the police. I'm making a citizen's arrest."

Petra arched an eyebrow at her. "Honey, I've known Tempest for years. She's a sweet little thing. And look at her cute dog. These two are never any trouble." She could lie so naturally when she needed to.

The woman's nose wrinkled. "That dog smells funny. She's probably not looking after him. We should take him to the pound."

I stepped up to the woman. "You touch one fur on Wiggles' head, and you'll be on the floor, just like Kirk."

She gaped at me and backed away, her cheeks flushing. "Did everyone hear that? She's threatening me now. I'll be dead next."

"Kirk's not dead!" At least I was pretty certain he wasn't. Was that amulet really so powerful? If it was, I needed to get out of here and find out.

Petra eased in between me and the shrill woman. "You're not exactly helping your cause," she muttered to me. "Your audience is out of control."

"You need to distract them," I said. "Frank wants to come out and play, and he'll destroy this place if he does."

"What do you want me to do?"

"Free drinks all around?"

Petra scowled at me. "You owe me for this."

Kirk groaned and rolled about on the floor.

I let out a relieved sigh. "There you go! He's not dead. I told you he just fainted."

Petra marched to the center of the bar. "Hey, everyone. Great news. Kirk's okay. Help him to the bar, so I can give him something to restore his strength."

The crowd didn't budge, and most of them were glaring at me.

"And the next round is on me," Petra said through gritted teeth.

That got them moving. Several people helped Kirk up, and he staggered about once he was on his feet.

"You hear that, Kirk?" someone said. "Free drinks for all the brave monster hunters."

Kirk groaned and swayed, his skin gray and blotchy.

I touched the amulet in my pocket. Should I give it back to him? Was this a healing amulet and I'd yanked it off, thinking it had something to do with him killing Sabine?

"Come on, big fella." Petra slid an arm through the elbow of the guy still blocking my way. "You don't want to miss out on a free drink."

He grunted at me before looking at Kirk. "I suppose he seems okay. I still think she did something weird to him."

"You'll forget all about that witch after you've had a drink." Petra winked at me. "Right this way."

I mouthed a thanks at her. I did owe Petra big time for this. I'd just reached the door when it was barged open, and Mom staggered in.

She grabbed my arm. "I'm so glad I found you. There's a problem."

I glanced around the bar. "Tell me about it. I was almost taken down by a mob of angry humans."

"Oh! No, that's not what I was talking about," Mom said. "Are you okay?"

"Fine. It's been handled. What's the problem with you?"

"It's Aurora's store. It's been broken into."

Chapter 19

I raced out of the Ancient Imp with Mom and Wiggles and over to Aurora's store.

"I've been keeping an eye on the place while she's away with Lex," Mom said. "The second I reached the door, I could tell something was wrong. I was certain I'd locked it yesterday, but it was open, and the magic wards to protect the store were broken."

"Someone broke through Aurora's wards? They'd need power to do that."

We reached the store, and I went in first to make sure no one was lurking in the shadows.

"I don't think anyone's in here. I checked before coming to find you," Mom said.

"Mom! You shouldn't have come in here on your own."

"I can handle myself when facing trouble. After all, I'm a Crypt witch."

I knew Mom could handle herself. She was a powerful witch, but that didn't mean I wouldn't always want to keep her safe.

I sucked in a breath as I took in the carnage in front of me. Shelves had been swept clean, and there were glass spell bottles broken everywhere.

Aurora's precious books had been yanked from the shelves and ripped apart.

Mom touched my arm. "Aurora will be devastated when she gets back. You know how much she loves this store."

I nodded. "Whoever did this, they wrecked the place. It seems almost malicious to do this much damage."

"It doesn't make any sense." Mom stepped over a heap of torn books. "Why cause so much mess? If they were looking for money, they'd have just gone for the register."

"Is there any money missing?" I scooped up Wiggles and set him on the counter, so he wouldn't get his paws injured by the broken glass.

"No, Aurora banked everything before going away. The float is in the safe, and that hasn't been touched."

I jammed my hands on my hips. "We need to clear this up and see if anything specific has been taken. That'll help us figure out why they broke in."

We spent the next few hours repairing books, clearing up broken bottles and scattered herbs, and fixing the shelves.

I went out back to make tea and see if Aurora had left any treats behind. I found a few oatmeal cookies, never my favorite, but they'd have to do. When I got back in the store, Mom was looking at a book on the counter.

"Did you find something interesting?" I set down the tea and cookies.

"A page has been torn from this spell book. Aurora would never damage her books. Whoever broke in must have taken it."

"Any idea which spell was taken?"

"Not yet. But it's in the section for devotion magic."

"You think someone was after a love spell?"

Mom pressed a hand flat against the book. "I don't think this attack has anything to do with love. Quite the opposite."

"Do you know who did this?"

She chewed on her bottom lip. "What if it was Zandra? She's been struggling to accept you and Aurora."

I didn't answer straight away. Zandra was impulsive, didn't have great control of her magic, and was jealous of Aurora and how perfect her life seemed to be. Could she be behind this attack? I'd hoped she'd gotten past her jealousy issues but maybe not.

"Do you know something about this?" Mom said. "Do you think Zandra would be so spiteful as to ruin the store?"

I had to believe in my half-sister. She wasn't this mean. "Zandra is having problems with her magic, but if the spell taken is an attachment or devotion spell, it makes no sense that this has anything to do with her. Who's she trying to make fall in love with her?"

Mom sighed. She picked up her mug and took a sip. "I don't want to think badly of her, and I understand she didn't have it easy growing up. It must have been difficult to grow into powers and not have anyone strong enough to train you."

Now Mom had put the idea in my head, I couldn't stop thinking that Zandra was a chaos maker. Her magic kept going awry, and she'd even rubbed Merrie the wrong way, and she was almost impossible to make angry. Could this be her work, too?

I shook my head. Zandra was struggling and wasn't finding it easy to accept her dad, our dad, had a whole other life she hadn't been involved in.

"What's the name of that book missing the spell?" I said.

"Advanced Magic Devotions." Mom read the name off the spine.

I hurried to the bookshelf where we'd placed the salvaged books. "There's another copy. We can see exactly which spell was taken." I returned to the counter and flipped it open.

Mom touched my arm. "I only want the best for the family. I don't want to think badly of Zandra. She's a part of our family. It's just... something I'm still adjusting to."

"Mom, I understand. I want Zandra to be a part of our family too, but I get how difficult it must be for you." My gaze went back to the book. "This is the missing page."

"Oh! That's bad if the thief took that." Mom shook her head as she read the spell. "It's the most powerful obsession spell you can create. It's hard to control and dangerous in the wrong hands. If an inexperienced magic user tried that on someone, it could kill both of them."

I skimmed through the ingredients list. There were a dozen items, including a rare type of astrid powder. "Aurora had a delivery of astrid root powder just before she went away. That's the key ingredient. If that's missing, then whoever broke into the store was after that and this spell."

"I'll check out the back," Mom said. She hurried away, while I waited by the counter, dunking a cookie into my tea to make it tastier.

"Who'd want to be-spell someone to make them obsess over you?" Wiggles sniffed my cookie and wrinkled his nose.

"Someone desperate. It's an unhealthy kind of love and not the kind anyone has any business dabbling in, especially if they don't know what they're doing."

"It's not here!" Mom hurried back, a smile on her face. "That's good news."

"It is?"

"It means Zandra didn't do this. All the powder's gone."

"That was supposed to last Aurora six months. That amount of powder would last a long time if they only used it in this spell. They'd be able to keep a person under an obsession spell for as long as they liked."

"Which would be bad for whoever was being controlled by the spell," Mom said. "It will damage them. They'd never be the same again."

I tapped my fingers on the counter. "Who'd be dumb enough to try this spell?"

"Someone lonely and looking for love?" Mom said.

"They must be desperate to risk doing this," I said. "And they must know we'd come after them when we discovered the store had been trashed."

"Unless it's not someone who lives here. We've got plenty of visitors in the village at the moment."

"Yes! And they've been riled up by Kirk. He's convincing them magic is real."

"It can't be a human with no spell experience. They'd struggle to make this spell work. They'd do more harm than good."

"Then they must have experience," I said.

"The village is full of tourists," Mom said. "How about focusing on couples? See if there is a couple walking around looking particularly loved up."

"Nice idea, but that would take too long. And tourists are coming and going all the time. Whoever did this could already have left the village with their newly obsessed partner by their side."

Mom closed the spell book in front of her. "Talking of partners, how are things going with Rhett?"

I shook my head. "It's not, but I can't think about him now. I've got too much going on."

Her expression of sympathy did nothing to help me feel better about my complicated situation with Rhett.

"Relationships take work," Mom said. "I wasn't sure I'd be able to forgive your dad for what happened, but I have."

I arched an eyebrow. "You're completely over that? You don't mind that Zandra's in our lives and possibly staying long term?"

"I... I was upset to begin with, but we figured things out. And I'm working through things when it comes to Zandra. The same will happen with you and Rhett. You'll find a solution if you're meant to be together."

I looked down at the book containing the obsession spells and shuddered. The weird things people did when it came to love baffled me. Maybe I was better off out of the relationship game.

But I couldn't focus on my own tangled love life. "Like you said, if it's meant to be, I'll work things out with him." My focus had to be elsewhere. I needed to figure out who killed Sabine, what was wrong with Kirk, and how someone dared break in to Aurora's store and believe they could get away with it.

Chapter 20

"Let's give this a few minutes to brew while I make pancakes." I stood from the couch in my apartment and rolled my shoulders. It was the morning after discovering Aurora's store had been broken into. After finishing the store clean-up with Mom, I'd had to head to work, but I was back on the case, trying to figure out what was going on with the amulet Kirk had around his neck.

Most of my experiments on the amulet had proved fruitless. It was refusing to give up its secrets, and that meant strong magic was involved.

I also had the half-dozen amulets Oakley had given me to test, but I was most interested in Kirk's magic. That was way more powerful.

"I could go for some pancakes," Wiggles said. "But you might like to open a window before you start cooking. It's getting pungent in here."

I cracked open a couple of windows. The herbs I'd been burning around the amulet to reveal its secrets did make for an interesting smell. It was a blend of swamp water, old cheese, and tobacco.

There was a knock on the door just as I was about to toss my first pancake.

Wiggles trotted over then backed away. "I smell angel outside."

I grimaced and gave the pancake a shake to loosen it. "That can't be good news. Maybe if we're quiet, they'll go away."

"Too late. I can hear you," Dazielle said. "Let me in."

Wiggles scurried away. "We could always jump out the window."

"Stop messing about. You're not in any trouble for once," Dazielle said.

I flipped the pancake then walked to the door and unlocked it. "Does this mean we're friends again if you're making social calls?"

"We're not friends. Tell me what happened with Kirk in the Ancient Imp."

"Um, how much do you know?" I stepped to one side and let her in.

"Fights, accusations, and attacks on humans. I've heard all kinds of stories." She arched an eyebrow. "What's your version of events, and why didn't you come tell me what you were doing?"

"I confronted Kirk about killing Sabine. He denied it. I didn't tell you because I didn't want to miss the chance to nab him and his dodgy magic."

"I have several reports from witnesses who say you attacked him." Dazielle crossed her arms over her chest and scowled at me. "We don't attack suspects we're investigating."

"I didn't attack Kirk, but things may have gotten out of hand. When I asked him what he knew about Sabine's murder, he didn't like it."

"Someone said you punched him in the throat," Dazielle said. "And I had another witness say you stole something from around his neck."

"I didn't punch him. Besides, he was fine when I left the Ancient Imp."

"He's far from fine. Kirk's in the hospital."

"Oh! I didn't know that. The last time I saw him, he was about to get a free drink, thanks to Petra." Okay, Kirk may have needed two people to hold him up, but he'd been awake and just about talking.

"Did you steal something from him?" Dazielle sniffed and her nose wrinkled. "What's burning?"

I grabbed the pan and groaned. My pancake was ruined. "That's your fault." I dumped the contents in the sink.

"I noticed you didn't deny stealing something from Kirk. What was it?"

I stared at my lost pancake. "An amulet."

"Is that what made him so ill?" Dazielle said. "Or did you use magic on him?"

"As tempting as it was to blast him into next year, I didn't touch Kirk. I figured the amulet I borrowed had magic in it. I needed to see what he was using."

"He was using a magic amulet?"

"Yes. He's using magic contained in amulets to trick people."

"You have proof of that?"

"Almost. I just need to unlock the amulet he was wearing to find out what he's been using. I think Sabine found out what he was doing. She either confronted him, and he needed to keep her quiet, or she decided to get in on the action. She had loads of amulets of her own; they're over there on the table. And, the first time I met her, Sabine revealed some amulets had gone missing from Kirk's collection. What if that was a cover? She could have taken them and pretended they'd been lost."

"Go back a few steps. Kirk was controlling people with magic?"

"Yes."

"And how was he mastering this magic? He has no ability."

"Which is probably why things started going wrong, and he got sick when I took the amulet from him."

Dazielle's brow wrinkled. "Sabine believed in magic enough to steal these amulets from Kirk? What did she plan to do with them?"

"I'll have to use a medium if you want me to ask her that question, but I'm sure Sabine had magic of her own. She talked to pixies as a child. And Bella mentioned she'd been adopted when she was young. Maybe she had magic from her biological parents and never knew it. Sabine must have seen something in the amulets and decided to take them. She could even have decided not to let Kirk keep exploiting magic for money. If she did, I'm in full support of that."

Dazielle exhaled slowly. "And you think Kirk found out and wasn't happy?"

"Exactly. This whole time, he's been using magic enhanced amulets to fool people. He must have used an amulet to create a fake alibi. He wasn't at Tilly's restaurant when Sabine was killed."

"Tilly's a strong witch. It would take more than a simple magic charm to fool her."

"I agree, but the amulet I grabbed from Kirk has a ton of power in it." I pointed at the table the amulet sat on. "Power it doesn't want to reveal. Power Kirk must have paid a lot for."

"That's the amulet you stole?"

"Borrowed."

"Stole."

"We'll disagree on that. I had to get a good look at it, and Kirk wasn't going to hand it over. He knew I was on to him."

Dazielle walked over and peered at the amulet. "If this is as powerful as you think it is, Kirk wouldn't have been able to control the magic."

"That's why he collapsed when I tore it off him."

"What have you found out about it?" Dazielle said.

"Not much. I've run numerous revelations spells and power reveal spells. It doesn't want to talk." My stomach grumbled. "Since you're here, do you want pancakes?"

"Not right now. Why is the amulet smoking?" Dazielle said.

"It is?" I dashed over to the table.

"It looks more like steam," Wiggles said. "And it doesn't smell too good. A bit like garbage after it's been left in the hot sun for too long."

Dazielle leaned closer. "I should take this to Angel Force. We can run tests on it there. Cassiel will be able to help."

"You need a witch to deal with this kind of magic," I said.

"My angels can deal with this. Witch magic isn't so special." She reached for the amulet.

"I wouldn't touch that," I said.

"I can handle your magic." Dazielle grabbed the amulet. There was a loud pop and a flash of bright light, and the amulet exploded.

When the smoke cleared, Dazielle stood with a shocked expression on her face and her eyebrows missing.

"You're on fire!" Wiggles knocked me to the ground and stamped on my stomach, putting out the flames that licked across my favorite sleep sweater.

I stared up at Dazielle as she remained frozen in place, horror on her face. "I told you that was intense magic." I petted Wiggles on the head before struggling to my feet.

"My face is numb." Dazielle's words were slurred. "What just happened?"

"The amulet must have had a self-destruct mechanism to hide the origins of the magic." I plucked at my charred sweater and frowned. It had taken me weeks to break it in so it was sleep soft.

Dazielle dabbed her fingers over her face. "I still feel odd. Do I look okay?"

"You'll be fine. Drink this." I handed her a full mug of coffee. "Your eyebrows won't take long to grow back."

Her hand flew to her brows. "My... eyebrows?"

"I can always magic them back on your face. Purple brows could be funky on you."

"Keep your magic away from me. How do I know you didn't make that amulet explode?"

"Dazielle, I can be a jerk, but I'm not that bad." I grabbed my own coffee and settled on the couch. "Whoever Kirk got that amulet from, he must have paid a lot to have something so powerful."

Dazielle sank onto the couch next to me, her hands shaking as she sipped her coffee. "He must have done. They've run tests on him at the hospital. He's a plain old human, not a magic bone in his body."

"Has Kirk said anything about the amulet?" I stared at the tiny fragments of smoldering amulet on the rug.

"He hasn't mentioned it, but he's having trouble forming sentences, so he's being kept sedated."

"It's weird. I pointed it out to him when we were talking, and he seemed confused, as if he wasn't even aware he was wearing it."

"I'm more interested in where he got it from. We have plenty of powerful magic users in the village," Dazielle said.

"No one here would be foolish enough to give Kirk that kind of power. We know the rules when it comes to humans and magic. It won't be anyone from here. Besides, Kirk goes around the country chasing magic creatures. He could have gotten that amulet anywhere."

"Which is no help to us. And with the amulet gone and Kirk not getting out of bed anytime soon, we're no closer to finding out who killed Sabine."

"Does this mean I'm back on the team?" I raised my mug to chink against Dazielle's.

She ignored my gesture. "We need to get Kirk talking."

"I can help with that, teammate. I'll get him to confess to Sabine's murder." I held my mug out again.

Dazielle slid me a glare. "Kirk does appear guilty." She touched her bare brows again.

"You could try penciling your brows back on. I'm sure I've got an old black eyebrow pencil somewhere. Or maybe a black marker pen would do."

"The barefaced look suits you," Wiggles said.

I stifled a laugh and downed my coffee. "Now you're convinced that Kirk's guilty, what's going to happen to Basil?"

"He'll be released. But he's still guilty of attacking those women," Dazielle said.

"Which he has admitted to. And he only did it because he was in mating mode. You should get him some therapy or sign him up to a dating agency so he can find a soulmate. Basil's just a lonely Bigfoot. He's not a threat to anyone."

"You're going soft."

"And you're getting mean. What's up with you?"

"Nothing. I'm taking his unusual situation into account, and it was his first offence, or at least he's never been caught before biting humans. It's unlikely he'll go to prison if he gets a sympathetic judge."

"Basil doesn't want to run around biting women. He's ashamed of what he's done. You find him the perfect match, and he'll be a reformed guy."

"I'm not playing matchmaker for Basil, but I will see he gets support with his compulsion issues."

I prodded a fragment of the amulet. There was a hint of power in there, but nothing I could work with. "I need to warn Oakley and Bella about this amulet and just how powerful it is."

"Why? What do they have to do with it?" Dazielle said.

"They're wearing amulets Kirk gave them. What if he's been controlling them with magic infused in the stones?"

"For what reason?"

"He didn't want them asking questions about Sabine, so he be-spelled them into silence."

"If that's the case, they could be in danger if the magic is becoming unstable." Dazielle stood, her wings fluttering. "I'll keep an eye on Kirk and see if I can get any sense out of him. You find Oakley and Bella and make sure they're safe."

I held out my hand for a fist bump. "You got it, partner."

Dazielle whacked me with a wing as she strode past. "Keep me informed." She slammed the door behind her.

"She's still grumpy," Wiggles said.

"And losing her eyebrows hasn't improved her mood." I grabbed my jacket. Breakfast would have to wait. "Let's move. We have some humans to protect."

Chapter 21

I dashed out of the apartment with Wiggles and was just in time to see Dazielle fly off. I ran to Tabitha Dimples' hotel to see if Oakley and Bella were in their rooms. "Hey, Tabitha! I'm looking for two of your guests, Oakley and Bella."

She smiled and pushed her glasses up her nose. "They're a charming couple. Always so polite. I've had no problems with them."

"I'm glad they're the perfect guests, but I have to see them. Which rooms are they in?"

"You won't find them here. They went for a walk half an hour ago. They've gone to look at the stone circle."

"Great. Thanks."

Tabitha's dark eyes narrowed. "Is there anything wrong? I'm usually an excellent judge of character, and I didn't pick up anything unusual about them."

"Hopefully not. See you later." I had no time to gossip with Tabitha, so I legged it back outside with Wiggles.

"Do you think Oakley and Bella are really in danger?" Wiggles bounded along beside me.

"If the same person created all these amulets, the chances are they linked the magic. There'd be a main amulet that contains most of the power and acts as the control."

"The one Dazielle blew up?"

"That's what I reckon. And it was the one Kirk was wearing to control everyone. He gave Oakley, Bella, and anyone else he felt needed one, an amulet so he could influence them. But Kirk got in over his head with this particular magic."

"But to use magic, you have to believe in it. Most humans only believe in it when they're small."

"I think Kirk does believe. He must have encountered magic when he was collecting artifacts for his exhibition. He could have stumbled across something he couldn't explain away. Once he got his head around the possibility of magic, he started to manipulate it." I was gasping by the time we got to the top of the hill and headed to the stone circle.

"There they are," Wiggles said.

I slowed as I spotted Oakley and Bella up ahead. Oakley was down on one knee and was holding Bella's hand. It looked like he was proposing to her.

I arrived just as Oakley stood, and Bella flung her arms around his neck and kissed him.

"Of course, I'll marry you," she said.

I staggered toward them, not believing what I was seeing. What the heck was going on? They were supposed to be friends. Oakley said he saw Bella as a buddy. What had changed between them so quickly?

"I hope I'm not interrupting an important moment," I said.

Bella's expression tightened for a second before she stepped back, keeping hold of one of Oakley's hands. "Tempest! We didn't expect anyone else to be around. If you don't mind, this is a private moment."

"Are congratulations in order?"

Bella grinned. "Oh, I guess we can tell you, and I'm just about bursting with happiness. This is so unexpected."

Oakley stared at Bella. He didn't look too good. He was sweating, and his skin was yellow.

"Oakley asked me to marry him," Bella said. "And I said yes!" She kissed his cheek.

"So I saw. You've had a big change of heart, Oakley," I said.

He scrubbed a hand down his face. "Yeah, I must have done. I... err... yeah, we're getting married?"

My gaze settled on the amulets around their neck as a horrible realization struck me. This whole time, I'd missed the truth about Sabine's so-called friends.

"Is there something you need, Tempest?" Bella said. "If not, we have to go celebrate our engagement."

"Yes, I've come to warn you that you're in danger."

"Danger? What's going on? Don't tell me the police let that wild creature loose." Bella's gaze flashed to the nearby woods.

"No, but you're in danger because of those amulets you're wearing. Where did you get them again?"

"Kirk gave them to us." Bella touched the amulet around her neck, and a small spark flew out of it and traveled up her arm.

I sucked in a breath. Her nice friend act was just that. She was behind all of this. The amulet she wore was the control, not the one that exploded.

"What's going on?" Oakley staggered to the side, only staying upright because Bella grabbed him.

"Nothing, my love. We'll be married soon, and you'll have nothing to worry about."

"You should worry about those stones around your neck. Kirk was wearing a similar amulet. When it was taken off, he collapsed," I said. "You need to get rid of them."

Oakley went to remove the amulet, but Bella smacked his hand down.

"An amulet can't make a person collapse. You're not making any sense," Bella said. "They're just trinkets."

"So take them off if they're not important."

Her eyes narrowed. "We need to leave, so we can tell our families the good news. They'll be so happy."

"About what?" Oakley said.

"Us getting married!" She shoved him. "Remember?"

"Oh, yeah. Getting married," Oakley said.

"You don't sound too happy about that," I said to Oakley. "Are you sure it's what you want? I thought you wanted to ask Sabine to marry you."

Oakley stared at me, his mouth open.

Bella turned a full-on scowl in my direction. "Of course, Oakley wants to marry me. We're best friends. Why shouldn't we be together?"

"Because Oakley loved Sabine. He wanted her as his wife. He came here in the hopes of reuniting with her. I expect you weren't happy when you learned about that."

Bella snorted a laugh. "You're mistaken. Oakley and I have been getting close for some time. He's been over Sabine for ages. Isn't that right?" She tugged on his hand.

Uncertainty flickered across Oakley's face. "Sabine's dead, isn't she?"

"That's right. So you can't marry her. And you're with me. It's how it's meant to be." Bella touched the amulet again, and another spark shot out of it and flew into her.

A swirl of worry spun through me. I'd been looking so hard at Kirk, convinced he'd killed Sabine, that I'd missed Bella. I'd believed her when she told me her alibi was Oakley, and all this time, she'd been the one using magic to exploit people.

"Where did you get those amulets, Bella?" I said. "And don't tell me it was from Kirk."

She shrugged. "Why do you care?"

"They contain powerful magic. Magic you don't know how to control."

"Magic! You sound almost as bad as Sabine. She always believed in that nonsense."

"You know it's not nonsense. You told me she used to see pixies. Could you see them too?"

"What's she talking about?" Oakley said.

"I have no idea, my love. She sounds jealous of our happiness."

"If you're genuine about each other, then I couldn't be more thrilled," I said. "But you're not. You're using magic to control people. Is that how you convinced Oakley to lie about where you were on the night of Sabine's murder?"

"Oakley, tell this woman we were together that night. You remember that."

"Um, I mean, I think we were." He scrubbed at his chin. "It's what you said happened."

"You remember it happening." Bella stroked his amulet and a flare of green light shot out and covered Oakley's face.

"Oh, of course. I remember now. We had a late dinner. We went to find Sabine, but she wasn't at work, so we went for a walk."

Oakley sounded robotic. He was clearly under the influence of Bella's magic.

"There you go," she said. "Now, we need to leave to celebrate our engagement."

"I thought you were sticking around to find out what happened to Sabine, or don't you care now you've got what you wanted?" I said.

Bella tugged on Oakley's hand. "Let's go."

He stumbled along behind her.

"You're not going anywhere," I said. "You murdered Sabine."

"Sabine's dead?" Oakley said.

"Be quiet," Bella said. "Stop talking. You're making him confused. Everything's fine. Sabine was killed by a wild animal, and Oakley and I are meant to be together. Sabine wouldn't want us grieving. She'd have wanted us to be happy."

"Sabine wouldn't have wanted you to kill her so you could have her ex-boyfriend. And you know Sabine wasn't killed by a wild animal. What were you doing, stalking around the woods until you could get Sabine on her own? You must have thought your luck was in when Basil bit her."

"Who's Basil?" Bella waved a hand in the air. "I don't care. We're going."

I stepped into her path. "You saw Sabine get bitten by a Bigfoot. She scared him away by screaming, but she was injured. Rather than helping her, you used that opportunity to kill her. Did she know it was you? Did you look in her eyes when you stabbed her in the neck? Did she even know why her best friend wanted her dead?"

"Bella, did you stab Sabine?" Oakley said, his eyes wide.

"No, my love. You need to rest. It's been an exciting morning, and you must be tired." Bella led Oakley to one of the large gray stones and pressed a hand against his amulet.

Oakley sank to the ground and didn't move.

Bella turned back to me, anger flaring in her eyes. "Stop interfering. This has nothing to do with you."

"You killed a woman in the place I live, and you tried to frame a friend of mine. You also made my uncle a suspect in this murder. That means I'm involved."

"It was that hairy ape thing that killed Sabine," Bella said. "What did you call it, a Bigfoot? Not that it matters. That thing deserves to be destroyed."

The amulet around her neck flared to life, and a pulse of dark, toxic magic drifted toward me.

I batted it away with a simple defense spell. "You planned this. Although I'm curious, weren't you stunned when you learned magic is real?"

"You should be locked up if you believe in magic. You're insane," Bella said.

"You'll be the one losing your mind if you keep using that amulet. And you must believe in magic, because you're manipulating Oakley with it. You do realize you'll have to use magic on him every day to convince him to stay with you? Spells fade if you don't refresh them."

"He's happy with me. He just needs... a reminder now and again."

"I'm assuming it was you who broke into my sister's magic store and stole the ingredients for an obsession spell? It doesn't look like it's working well, though. Oakley isn't thrilled to be engaged to you."

"Once I have everything under control, Oakley will love me."

"You can't use magic to force someone to do something that's not natural to them. It'll only be a temporary effect, and you'll drive him insane if you force him into this relationship. The spell you used is powerful, and it'll destroy you and him. Humans using magic is unnatural. You must feel the impact of that amulet. It'll change you."

"You do sound just like Sabine. She was convinced there was a price to pay when it came to magic, but she still used it to invite those terrifying little pixie things into her garden."

"Your imaginary friends were real. You could see them?"

Bella shuddered. "I could. And I was horrified when she introduced me to them. They were mean, but I did everything they told me because I was terrified they'd eat me in my sleep. Sabine thought they were amazing."

"Sabine had magic? She didn't buy spells or trinkets to make the magic work?"

Bella lifted her chin. "No. She could do weird stuff when we were kids. She used to have this fantasy that her witch mom would find her one day and take her somewhere magical. As we grew older, it got embarrassing. We had a fight about it after she scared away a guy I liked with some dumb story about witches. I told her we couldn't be friends if she kept being a freak. She didn't do anything weird after that, and I was glad."

"What ability did she have?"

Bella snorted a laugh. "Sabine could see magic creatures. She could even do a basic spell, nothing difficult, but she could make a flower bloom and had an affinity with animals. It wasn't until she finished her history degree and started working with Kirk that her passion for magic ignited again. She even confided in me that she wanted to learn a few spells."

"And that's when you decided to give magic a go too? You figured, if it worked for Sabine, why not you? And you knew exactly what you wanted to get with that magic: Oakley."

"I saw no harm in doing a simple love spell. Not that I believed in it, but I'd tried everything else to get him to notice me. I got him drunk and tried to seduce him. I pretended to fall asleep in his bed so he'd find me. I even told him Sabine didn't want him and would never get back with him. Nothing worked. He kept obsessing over her."

"So you had to get rid of Sabine. You decided to kill her because, once she was out of the picture, Oakley would notice you."

"We're so good together," Bella said. "He just needed to see that and move on from Sabine."

"You must have been gutted when he told you he wanted to get back with her. Did Oakley let you know he was planning to ask Sabine to marry him?"

"He did. I thought he was an idiot."

"But you still wanted him."

Bella screeched at me, and the amulet sparked. It looked like it was feeding off her anger.

"Take off the amulet before you get hurt," I said.

"Leave us alone. We could be happy together. I know it. You're not spoiling my happily ever after." She lunged at me, magic sparks flickering around her like she was a giant sparkler.

I dodged her attack, and Bella stumbled past me and almost landed on her face. It wouldn't take much to knock her down, but I needed to hold back my magic. If I used too strong a spell, it could rip away what was left of her sanity.

Bella whipped her hands forward, and black flames blasted toward me.

I reared back, so surprised by the power in that magic that it almost got me, and heat seared past my skin.

She had some nasty power flowing through her, and it would destroy her if I didn't get that amulet off her neck.

My own magic called for me to ruin her. Bella was trouble, and she'd brought trouble to my village. I wasn't certain if Frank was influencing my desire to kill, but I reined in my urge. I'd protect myself, Wiggles, and Oakley and make sure Bella didn't mess with anyone else, but no one needed to die.

Bella leaped closer, landing in a crouch and baring her teeth.

"That's impressive. Did you learn that move from the movies?" I sparked a warning of magic on my fingers. "If you keep fighting, you'll die."

"You'd kill me?"

"No, you'll kill yourself. Take off the amulet. The second you stop letting that magic control you, you'll feel better."

Bella's magic flared around her like a wild tornado, and she snarled.

"We should let her burn herself out," Wiggles said. "The way that power has a hold on her, she's too late to save."

"Then she'll get away with murder."

"I knew there was something weird about that mangy dog." Bella charged at me.

I raised my hand and shoved it forward, sending out a blast of freezing water. That would cool her rage.

She screamed and slammed into me, taking us down. Her hands latched onto my throat. "I did kill Sabine, and I was glad to do it. She didn't deserve

Oakley. He was mine, and I was determined to have him."

I ripped the amulet off Bella's neck, tossed it in the air, and threw a fireball at it. It exploded in a shower of multi-colored sparks, singeing us as they floated down.

Bella groaned and flopped onto the dirt as the magic left her, her eyelids fluttering.

Oakley gave a garbled moan. "What's going on? Why am I here?" He stared at me with bleary eyes.

"Go check he's okay," I said to Wiggles. "And get that amulet off his neck before it blows."

Wiggles trotted over, ripped the amulet away and stamped on it before setting it on fire. "It's all good here. How's Bella doing?"

I looked down at Bella. Her eyes were rolling, and she was turning gray. "Not so great, but she's still under arrest for murder."

Chapter 22

"I wish they'd hurry up and leave." Dazielle glowered at the dawdling tourists as they headed through the barrier and out of Willow Tree Falls.

"What's eating you? You're not usually so snappy at our visitors. You're always telling me the village has to welcome everyone." I stood from petting Wiggles and leaned against the wall.

She worked her jaw from side to side. "I've had to pay my angels overtime since they've been here. It doesn't do my budgeting any favors. And I have extra reports to complete, thanks to Kirk and his meddling in magic."

"Speak of the devil." I couldn't help but smirk as Kirk staggered toward us. It had been two days since Bella was arrested for killing Sabine. Not only had she been charged with murder, but she was also in trouble for breaking into Aurora's store and be-spelling Oakley and Kirk. Yep, she'd given them both amulets to make sure Kirk caused maximum chaos while she tried to get away with murdering her best friend.

Two trucks rumbled past, their engines groaning as they struggled to contend with the magic messing with their components. One of them pulled up as Kirk stopped next to me and Dazielle.

His scowl showed just what he thought of us. "I haven't finished with this place."

"You really should be finished with it," I said.

"I know there's something odd about this village. I will find out what it is." Kirk looked like he hadn't slept in days, and I did feel a flicker of sympathy for him, even though he was a huge jerk. Humans and magic really shouldn't tangle.

"Have a safe journey home," Dazielle said, her tone way too sweet to be genuine.

Kirk frowned as he pulled open the passenger door to the truck and jumped in.

The truck lurched a few feet before the engine died. I watched with amusement as it refused to start.

Kirk and the driver climbed out and had to push the truck through the magic barrier. It was a barrier they couldn't see, but their truck definitely could feel. The second the magic no longer affected it, the engine roared to life, and they disappeared.

"They'd better not come back," I said.

"It would be sensible if Kirk took a long break from interfering with magic."

"I agree with that."

"Although when he was in the hospital recovering, he was mumbling about some aunt who had abilities, so he could have seen magic happening when he was a kid. And maybe there's a faint trace of it running through him."

"But that doesn't mean he knows how to control it," I said.

Several more groups of visitors walked past us as we were talking. The village finally felt like it was returning to normal. The killer had been caught, justice was done, and we were due a few weeks of quiet.

Oakley strolled over, a bag slung over one shoulder.

"You're leaving too?" I said to him.

He nodded. "There's nothing left for me here. Not now Sabine's gone, and, well, now I know the truth about Bella. I can't believe she messed with me. I still can't figure out how she convinced me to propose."

"It was most likely drugs," I said. "She probably slipped something into your drink. There's some strong stuff out there."

He scrubbed at his stubbled chin. "It could be that. I never knew she liked me in that way, though. It's too weird."

A repair truck rumbled past with his car on the back.

Oakley frowned. "That's another thing I need to deal with. Do you know any good garages around here?"

"You should give it a try once you're a little way out from the village," I said. "The lay lines around here do weird things to vehicles."

His forehead wrinkled. "Lay lines? Sabine used to talk about those. They're something magical?"

"No!" Dazielle glared at me. "They're part of the earth's magnetic core."

"And they're strong enough to mess with engines?"

"You got it." I grinned at him. "And you know this place; all sorts of weird things go on."

Oakley glanced around. "I should take a look through Sabine's things, see if she left behind any clues about this magic stuff. I could pick up where she left off."

"My advice would be to move on and forget all about it," Dazielle said.

Oakley shrugged. "You could be right. I'd better get going. Thanks for helping with everything." He strode away.

"You shouldn't encourage someone to dabble in magic," Dazielle said. "You saw what happened to Kirk and Bella."

"I reckon Oakley has a little magic in him. And he's an open-minded guy. Besides, he needs something to occupy him now he's lost the woman he loved and his best friend."

"You should have told him to take up jogging, not magic."

The last of the crowds headed away from the village.

I let out a sigh. "Peace at last."

We'd just turned back to the center of the village, when Basil slipped out from behind a cottage and hurried over. "I wanted to see you to say goodbye before I left."

"Hey, Basil. Have you taken a look at those profiles I sent you? The supernatural dating agency has had a lot of success. It could be the perfect way to find a mate," I said.

He grinned at me. "They look great. I've already arranged to meet three of them."

"No biting, unless you have their permission," Dazielle said. "You're lucky not to be going to prison."

Basil raised a hand. "I know. And I appreciate you speaking up for me. I promise I'm working on my control issues."

"And don't forget your weekly mandatory therapy sessions," Dazielle said. "If you miss a single one, I will arrest you."

"I'll go to them. I promise."

"Good luck in finding your perfect match," I said.

"Thanks. And thank your Uncle Kenny for everything he did for me. He's a good guy, and if he ever wants to know more about Bigfoot, he has my details."

We said our goodbyes, and Basil headed out of Willow Tree Falls.

"A dating agency," Dazielle said. "I didn't have you down as a matchmaker."

"The poor guy needed help. We don't want him getting too amorous and biting women when his lust is up."

Dazielle grumbled under her breath.

"What gives with you? You've been a nightmare to work with on this case. You have to tell me what's wrong."

"No, I haven't."

"You've been a grouch," Wiggles said. "A big old, feathered, snarly, mean grumpy face."

Dazielle scowled at him. "That's because you and Tempest bring out the worst in me."

I shook my head. "And what have you got against all the guys in the village? You had it in for Uncle

Kenny and Tate, and they've never done anything bad to you."

"They were suspects in a murder investigation."

"Stop reeling out that line. It's not true. And you had no legitimate reason to go after Tate. Okay, Uncle Kenny was found at the murder scene covered in blood, but I know something else is wrong."

Dazielle huffed out a breath. "My mom will soon be visiting."

"That's a bad thing?"

"She has a specific reason for visiting."

"And you're not happy about that reason?" She was making me work to get the information out of her.

Dazielle stared off into the distance. "Mom is planning my wedding."

Wiggles snorted out a bark-laugh, and a flame shot out of his mouth, almost hitting Dazielle's foot. "You're getting married?"

"Don't sound so surprised," Dazielle said. "I'm considered a catch."

"I didn't even know you were dating." I nudged Wiggles away with my toe as he continued to snort laugh. "Who's the lucky guy?"

"I've known him a long time. It was arranged when we were children. Let's just say he hasn't developed into the kind of man I want in my life full time."

"That's the reason you've been so down on all the guys around here?"

"I'd never do anything so childish," Dazielle said.

I chuckled. "You need to stop seeing all men as the enemy. If you don't like the guy, break it off with him."

"It's not that simple. When angels enter into an understanding, it can be difficult to break. And my mom's determined a wedding will go ahead. She's demanding it."

"Dazielle, she won't want you getting married to someone you don't like. Stop grouching at everyone and ditch this loser. Besides, I always figured you were a strong, independent angel who didn't need a man in her life."

"So did I," she muttered.

I grinned. Dazielle's life was about to get a lot more interesting, and I couldn't wait to see how that panned out.

We made our way slowly back toward Angel Force.

"My mood hasn't been helped because you're so difficult to work with," she said.

"That's a glowing endorsement. You've certainly been a challenge recently."

"If you let me finish, I'll admit that you did figure out this case."

Oh! So, this was Dazielle trying to be nice to me. I'd take it. I'd even throw her a bone. "I did, eventually. Once I stopped obsessing over Kirk."

"I can understand why you did that. He was a jerk."

"Yep. He absolutely was." I nudged her with my elbow. "We can both be stubborn, and we always think we're right. It makes for a complicated working relationship."

"I suppose all that matters is the killer got what she deserved."

I nodded. "About people getting what they deserve, have you reconsidered firing Dominic? He has a heart of gold. He'd never put information on that blog if he thought it would hurt anyone."

"But it did hurt someone. And it brought Kirk to the village. That's unforgivable."

"You're being too hard on him. Dominic is always desperate for a kind word from you, so when Kirk manipulated him by telling him he was clever, he lapped it up. You're not blameless here."

"I should have sacked him a long time ago," Dazielle said. "He's not cut out for Angel Force."

"Dominic is great with people, he always has a smile on his face, and he likes to keep tense situations calm. Maybe he's not got a brilliant mind, but he just wants to be helpful."

"I've experienced plenty of Dominic's help over the years. He should try a different career path."

"He'll be lost without Angel Force. Although I am curious as to how he got his blog up and running. No computer would last five minutes in the village before its components fry."

"He took trips out of Willow Tree Falls and rented time on a computer in a café."

"You see! He showed initiative. And he must have great research skills. Give Dominic another go."

She walked along without speaking for a long time. "I'll think about it."

I checked the time. "I need to get out of here. I've got a big family lunch today." Dad had finally arranged for Zandra to meet everyone, and Mom had been flapping ever since, suggesting all kinds of extravagant food. We'd finally settled on keeping it simple and were having lunch at my parents' house.

"I need to go too," Dazielle said. "I have to have a long conversation with my mom about wedding dresses."

I managed to conceal my laugh behind a cough. "Have fun." I strode away with Wiggles beside me.

"Dazielle as the blushing bride, I never thought I'd see that," Wiggles said.

"An angel wedding. That's got to be extravagant. I imagine it'll feature lots of white and feathers. I do get now why Dazielle's been so snappy. I'd be miserable if I was being forced to marry someone I didn't like."

We turned the corner, and I raised my hand as I spotted Zandra lurking outside the gate of my parents' home.

"What are you doing waiting out here on your own?" I said.

Zandra tugged the hem of her shirt. "This is a bad idea."

I caught hold of her elbow before she could escape. "Don't fail me now. You were the one complaining that you didn't feel part of this family. You're ready for this. And going through the initiation of lunch with everyone is a crucial part of being involved."

"I didn't say I wasn't ready. I'm not scared." She tilted her chin, worry clear in her eyes.

I wrapped my arm around her shoulders and gave her a squeeze. I kept forgetting how young Zandra was. As much as she tried to brazen it out, she was bound to be freaking out about meeting everyone.

"Let's go inside. Most of them don't bite, although watch out for Auntie Queenie's familiar. She can nip you if she's in a bad mood."

Zandra nodded and chewed on her bottom lip as we headed through the gate.

"And a word of warning, don't let Granny Dottie get you drunk and watch out for her collard greens. She covers them in chili powder because she thinks it makes them taste better." I poked my tongue out.

Zandra smirked. "Got it."

We stopped at the front door, and I put my hand on the doorknob. "Deep breaths. It'll be fine. They'll love you."

Zandra's gaze cut to the gate. She swallowed then nodded. "I can handle a boring family lunch. There's nothing to it."

I laughed as I opened the door. "Trust me, there's never a boring moment when you're a Crypt witch." I led her into the house, the inviting smell of roast potatoes and apple pie drifting up my nose.

It was time for a new challenge, and this one involving my whole family.

About Author

K.E. O'Connor (Karen) is a cozy mystery author living in the beautiful British countryside. She loves all things mystery, animals, and cake. When she's not writing about mysteries, murder, and treats, she volunteers at a local animal sanctuary, reads a ton of books, binge-watches mystery series, and dreams about living somewhere warmer.

To stay in touch with the fun mysteries:

Newsletter:
www.subscribepage.com/cozymysteries

Website:
www.keoconnor.com

Facebook:
www.facebook.com/keoconnorauthor

Also By

Luck of the Witch
Hell of a Witch
Revenge of the Witch
Curse of the Witch
Son of a Witch
Framing of the Witch
Trickery of the Witch
Wishes of the Witch
Harmony of the Witch
Remedy of the Witch
Gift of the Witch
Toil of the Witch
Jinxing of the Witch
Craving of the Witch
Union of the Witch
Chaos of the Witch
Sleighing of the Witch

If you enjoyed

Craving of the Witch

turn the page to read an extract from the next Crypt Witch Mystery

UNION OF THE WITCH

To learn more about the series, scan your country-specific QR code.

Chapter 1

"Keep your head down, or the demon will see us and make a run for it, and I'm not chasing him all over town." I crouched beside my half-sister, Zandra.

We'd been skulking around the shadowy alleyways in Mudacre for three hours, and there was nothing pleasant about this place. It was a strip of gambling dens, cheap bars, and greasy looking takeout joints. Even Wiggles would turn up his nose at the pizza on offer if he was here.

"Paxos isn't going to show." Zandra's scowl looked scarily similar to mine when I realized I'd run out of brownies *and* the cookie tin was empty.

"You don't know that for sure. And this is your chance to learn the business. You can put your magic to good use by bringing down demons as my side-kick."

"Side-kick! You'll be my side-kick if my power keeps growing."

She wasn't wrong. Zandra had a natural ability for the darker shades of magic. And as an untrained witchling, that could mean trouble for anyone who got in her way.

"Besides, I already put my magic to good use." She shuffled along beside me, kicking aside a broken chunk of brick.

"Stop making so much noise. Anyone would think you don't want to find this demon and arrest him."

"Maybe I don't. What's wrong with demons, anyway?"

"Oh, I don't know. They terrorize innocent people, they have a tendency to flay, dismember, and destroy at a moment's notice, and they leave piles of foul-smelling goo everywhere. They also—"

"Yeah, yeah. I get the point. Witches are awesome and demons are bad." Her gaze ran over me.

I adjusted the demon catching bag hanging off my belt loop. "Have you got something on your mind?"

"Well, you know, Frank and all." She gestured at me. "I figured you must have some affinity with demons, since you've been carrying one around for so long. Some of that demon badness must have rubbed off on you along the way."

"Nope. Frank rubs no part of me. And if he ever did, I'd have myself magically deep cleansed. And having an unwanted demon lodger inside me doesn't mean I'm making friends with other demons. Now, focus! What are the five tips I've told you when you're on a demon hunt?"

"Something about pizza and blah, and blah de blah blah. And I forget the rest."

I groaned. Zandra made a terrible student. Not only had she reverted to acting like a fourteen-year-old, she hadn't listened to a word I'd said about how to track a demon and cause the least amount of damage when capturing it.

I wrinkled my nose. We were so similar that it was painful to witness. Had I really been that bad when learning how to perfect the art of demon hunting?

Most likely.

But I wasn't going easy on Zandra. She'd crossed the line recently and misused magic. I had to put a stop to that before it got noticed by the wrong people, or more specifically, the wrong angels, and she got arrested.

"I see something up ahead." Zandra shot out a light ball.

I killed it instantly and grabbed her by her collar. "Stop joking around. We only use spells around non-magicals in an emergency."

"I figured that spotting a demon was an emergency." She struggled out of my grip and stepped away. "Haven't we done enough demon hunting for one night?"

"We don't stop hunting until we find this thing. Paxos put six people in the hospital."

"Six non-magical people in the hospital."

"And your point?"

"They... err... well, wasn't it their fault they got hurt? They got in his way."

"He barreled through a funeral, stole the corpse from the open casket, and punched twenty people. And he set the chapel alight and vomited goo all over the wake buffet. This is a bad demon. He needs stopping."

"Let the angels deal with him. We're out of boring Willow Tree Falls for once. Let's go have fun. We could try out a casino. I know a few spells that guarantee we'd walk away winners."

"What's so boring about our home?"

Zandra kicked at the ground. "It might be your home, but it's not mine."

"Sure it is. You've been there for months. It can be quiet at times, but I like it."

"I only stay around because I haven't had a better offer."

I grabbed Zandra's arm and yanked her behind a huge dumpster. A second later, a huge pile of gray demon goo landed where she'd been standing.

Zandra's eyes were wide with excitement as she stared at the goo. "Let's go grab ourselves a demon."

"Wait! Not so fast. Take a good look at the goo deposit."

"I'm not poking around in demon muck. I don't know which hole that goo came out of."

"Look at it. Demons emit different secretions in a range of colors."

Zandra nudged the lump of goo with her foot. "I'm guessing this is some kind of demon with a bad head cold."

"Gray goo doesn't come out of the demon we're hunting. When Paxos is angry, he spits out a shower of orange goo. Don't get that on your skin or it'll burn."

Zandra glanced up. "We've been tracking the wrong demon all this time?"

"No. I know how to track demons. All this shows is that there are more of them on the loose than we realized. And sometimes, the demons just like to hang out in dark alleyways, make scary noises, and dump muck on people's heads for fun."

"Which is annoying but not exactly terrifying," Zandra said.

"It depends. If you were trying to get to sleep while some creepy thing with claws and a tail tapped on your window and spat goo at you, you'd be terrified."

Zandra shuddered. "Give me nightmares, why don't you?"

"And imagine not being able to defend yourself with magic? That's why we're out here."

"We should just use magic to find him. Throw out a few detection spells, and we can grab ourselves a demon. Maybe we could get them both. Do we get a bonus if we snag more than one demon?"

"Nope. All we'd do was annoy Dazielle if we brought back the wrong demon."

"It doesn't take much to annoy her. She's always snappy."

I nodded. Dazielle had a stressful job heading up Angel Force, but she had been a giant pain over the last few months. I'd been keeping out of her way until she'd offered me a paid gig hunting Paxos.

"How about this? If we catch the demon, we can take the rest of the night off," Zandra said.

I gritted my teeth as I stalked along the alleyway. I'd hoped that bringing Zandra with me on demon hunting missions would give her a positive channel for her magic, maybe even inspire her to become a demon hunter and use that spiky magic she struggled to control for something positive. But she wasn't interested.

"This is boring," Zandra muttered as she caught up with me. "Why drag me out with you to do something so dull? I don't see you bringing Aurora on demon hunting missions."

"There are two problems with having Aurora here." I pointed to my chest. "One is the demon inside me who wants to grab her and make her his plaything. And Aurora's magic is pure. It's about positivity and bringing people joy. Demons don't want joy. They want destruction. They react badly to happiness."

"You're saying my magic isn't pure?"

I arched an eyebrow at Zandra. "You've had your moments since you moved to Willow Tree Falls. You're more a blast first and ask questions later kind of witch."

"And that's a bad thing? It's kept me alive this long."

"It's a bad thing if you attract the attention of Angel Force."

"I can outrun those feathered idiots. Or out-blast them with magic if I have to."

There'd been a time when I'd thought exactly the same thing about the angels. And most of the time, they were still pretty idiotic, but I had a decent bond with some of them, and I'd learned it was never wise to ruffle their feathers. For all their angelic smiles and soft fluffy wings, they packed a powerful magical punch.

"Let's keep looking for our demon," I said.

"Only if you agree we can take a break in half an hour. My feet are aching."

"Sure. If we've not found any signs of Paxos, we'll grab snacks from the least dodgy looking takeout place."

Zandra worried me. She hadn't had the best upbringing, but I was determined to make sure she didn't fly off the rails and get herself in trouble. But sometimes, she skated too close to the dark side of magic, and I wasn't certain I'd be able to catch her if she tipped off track.

Twenty minutes of pointless alleyway searching later, we were still no closer to finding Paxos.

"Let's take that break," I said. "What snacks do you want?"

Zandra grinned and bounded along the alleyway, swinging her arms. "Ice cream."

"It's freezing out here. How about hot chocolate?"

"We could go for hot fudge sundaes? There must be a place around here that's still open. An all-night diner that does dessert. I'll cast a—"

"No! No spells." I checked the time. It was two in the morning. The only places around here that would still be open were dodgy bars and clubs.

I rounded the corner and walked straight into Zandra, who'd stopped dead on the sidewalk.

She grabbed my arm and yanked me back.

"Did you see the demon?" I whispered.

Her eyes were wide as she shook her head. "No, someone much more interesting. Take a look and see for yourself."

I peered around the corner and scanned the quiet street. It took a minute, but then I spotted a figure skulking in the shadows on the opposite side of the road. He was tall, wore black jeans and a leather jacket with the collar turned up. My heart bounced down to my toes and back up into my chest.

"That's Rhett, isn't it? The guy who ditched you for his buddies and left Willow Tree Falls without even saying goodbye," Zandra whispered in my ear.

I winced. That hit too close to home. "That's not exactly what happened." It was exactly what happened. Rhett left after an argument we'd never resolved, and I hadn't seen him since.

"The way I heard it, he showed up for Aurora's fancy wedding and then vanished on you," Zandra said. "He didn't even ask you to dance at the reception. What a jerk."

"He has his moments. Don't we all?" I huffed out a quiet breath as I continued to watch Rhett. *What was he doing here?*

A finger jabbed into my ribs.

"Ouch! Quit doing that." I glared at Zandra.

"It is true, though. He did walk out on you?"

"It's sort of true. It's also complicated." I felt abandoned by Rhett. I hadn't seen him for ages and had almost given up on him.

My treacherous little heart was bumping away like it had just had an electric shock, making me think all kinds of dumb thoughts like running after him or rationalizing that there must have been an emergency for him to leave so suddenly. It would all make sense once he'd explained everything to me, like I was a needy girlfriend with no life of my own.

Rhett hadn't even sent me a message to say goodbye. He'd simply upped and left, leaving our relationship in tatters. I didn't even know if I was single since we hadn't officially ended things. I felt very single, but I couldn't deny the way my heart pounded at seeing him again.

"What do you think he's doing lurking about in a dump like this?" Zandra said.

"I've no idea." I hadn't realized it, but I'd moved out of the alleyway and was standing on the street corner.

"Tempest! Let's follow him," Zandra said. "Don't you want to know what your shady ex-boyfriend has been getting up to? I would if he was mine."

My eyes narrowed. "You're too young to have a serious boyfriend." I couldn't tear my gaze away from Rhett. He was making sure no one paid him any attention as he slid from shadow to shadow, his head down and his gaze on the sidewalk.

"Stop treating me like a kid. I'm only a few years younger than you."

"Which is still young. And dating leads to trouble. My advice is not to do it."

"You mean the kind of trouble you find yourself in by creeping around dark alleyways after your missing boyfriend?"

"Exactly." I took a step in the direction Rhett was walking then stopped. What was I doing? I wasn't the kind of woman who chased after a guy.

"You're desperate to find out what Rhett's up to." Zandra grabbed my arm and hurried me along the sidewalk. "I won't tell anyone we followed him. It'll be our secret."

"It won't be a secret, because that's not what we're doing." Still, I kept walking. It seemed I had treacherous feet and a treacherous heart.

"Isn't he usually with his gang?" Zandra said.

"They're probably around here somewhere."

"Doing something they shouldn't?"

I shrugged. Rhett's biker gang walked a murky gray line when it came to illegal activities. Since he'd taken over the gang leadership, he'd calmed the group, and they mainly stayed on the straight and narrow, but none of them were angels, Rhett included.

Zandra yanked my arm so hard, she almost dislocated it. "Is that his bike?"

I pulled my arm away from her painful grip and rolled my shoulder. "It looks like it."

"I've been testing out a flying spell. I could use it on both of us. We could tail him from the air. He wouldn't know we were after him." She touched her palms together and sparks of magic flew from her fingertips.

I grabbed her hand and squeezed until the magic faded. "No flying spells. No magic of any kind while we're in the open."

Zandra rolled her eyes. "Don't you want to know what he's up to? This would be killing me. I'd have to know."

My gaze lifted as Rhett's bike roared to life and he zoomed away. Of course I wanted to know what he was doing. But I didn't chase after any guy, no matter our history or how gorgeous he was. Rhett had let me down big time, and if he ever crawled back to Willow Tree Falls with his gang, he'd have a lot of making up to do. And even then, I wasn't sure I'd be interested in him. He'd need more than a bunch of flowers to sort out this mess.

I tilted my head and breathed in deeply. The stench of overripe fruit, gone off meat, and stale beer filled my nose. My gaze shifted to the alleyway opposite us, and I caught a flash of scales and teeth.

"I've got something much more interesting than my old boyfriend to deal with," I said. "Do you smell that?"

Zandra lifted her nose and took a deep breath. "The overripe banana and gross meat smell?"

"That's our demon. Let's go have a good old-fashioned brawl with a bad guy."

"That might make you feel better after seeing Rhett ride off without even noticing you."

I almost growled at her. Instead, I channeled my anger into my magic. This poor sap of a demon wouldn't know what had hit him.

Union of the Witch is available in paperback and e-book.